It was an argument they could have later, assuming they survived the next few minutes...

"Ready, Becca?"

"One second." She fisted her hands in his jacket panels and pulled Parker close. Her lips met his with an urgency that shot through his veins like a bolt of lightning.

He wrapped his arms around her, bringing her flush against his body. At last, he indulged the fantasy of claiming her mouth. Becca's lips parted and his tongue stroked across hers. The pleasure and heat wove a spell around him. Parker ran his hands up over her ribs, his thumbs following the soft curve of her breasts.

The soundtrack of heavy boots thundering on the stairs brought him slamming back to reality. Breaking the kiss, Becca's taste lingering on his tongue, he pushed open the door and they ran...

RELUCTANT HERO

USA TODAY Bestselling Authors

DEBRA WEBB
&
REGAN BLACK

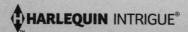

HARLEQUIN INTRIGUE®

For my dad, the first hero in my life, who nurtured my independence and taught me to believe without limits. —Regan

Recycling programs for this product may not exist in your area.

ISBN-13: 978-1-335-72134-1

Reluctant Hero

Printed in U.S.A.

www.Harlequin.com

Debra Webb, born in Alabama, wrote her first story at age nine and her first romance at thirteen. It wasn't until after she spent three years working for the military behind the Iron Curtain—and a five-year stint with NASA—that she realized her true calling. Since then the *USA TODAY* bestselling author has penned more than one hundred novels, including her internationally bestselling Colby Agency series.

Regan Black, a *USA TODAY* bestselling author, writes award-winning, action-packed novels featuring kick-butt heroines and the sexy heroes who fall in love with them. Raised in the Midwest and California, she and her family, along with their adopted greyhound, two arrogant cats and a quirky finch, reside in the South Carolina Low Country, where the rich blend of legend, romance and history fuels her imagination.

Books by Debra Webb and Regan Black

Harlequin Intrigue

Investigating Christmas
Marriage Confidential
Reluctant Hero

Colby Agency: Family Secrets

Gunning for the Groom
Heavy Artillery Husband

The Specialists: Heroes Next Door

The Hunk Next Door
Heart of a Hero
To Honor and To Protect
Her Undercover Defender

Visit the Author Profile page at Harlequin.com for more titles.

CAST OF CHARACTERS

Rebecca (Becca) Wallace—The only daughter of a Hollywood film-studio mogul, time and again she has proven she has the skills to back up the reputation of her family name. Now, as producer for a highly acclaimed investigative program on a national network in San Francisco, she has been tipped off to a scandal that could ruin the reputations of the US Army and several former soldiers.

Parker Lawton—After his service with the US Army, he returned home to open and operate a private investigations and security company in San Francisco. The cofounders of Gray Box are among his top clients. Now it seems enemies from his military career have followed him home.

Rush Grayson—Friend of Parker and cofounder of Gray Box, an online service that is considered the best option for storing data in the information-security industry. Newly married to Lucy Gaines.

Lucy Gaines Grayson—A new addition to the Gray Box team, Lucy brings a fresh viewpoint and energy the executive staff appreciates. Newly married to Rush Grayson.

Sam Bellemere—Friend of both Parker and Rush and cofounder of Gray Box, Sam developed the unique "hack-proof" software and handles ongoing cybersecurity for the company.

Chapter One

Rebecca Wallace had an itch between her shoulder blades, warning her it was well past time to get out of the office. She'd turned off the three monitors on the wall, all of them muted, that were tuned to the television network she worked for and their top two competitors. She scrolled her mouse over to power down her computer when a new email icon popped up on her monitor.

She should ignore it. Needed to ignore it. She had a date tonight—the first in months—and she already knew she was going to be late. Late wasn't a behavior she tolerated in others, so she did her best to be prompt as often as possible. Her career as a producer for an acclaimed investigative journalism show frequently put her at odds with her aim to be on time.

While the weekly show was scheduled down to the second, when important stories broke, she felt an obligation to be available to support the stable of reporters the network had in the field.

Knowing the news cycle had wound down for the day, she exercised self-discipline and shut down the computer. She would read the email on her phone during the commute home and then delegate any response if necessary. With a longing glance at her laptop, she left it behind as well. Carving out a personal life had been one of her primary intentions for this year. Considering this was only her tenth date for the year and it was October, she scolded herself for letting an important goal slide.

Deciding the email would wait until the morning, she set her phone to vibrate and dropped it into her purse. Her team had the next big story in the works already. Last week, she and her lead journalist, Bill Gatlin, had started digging into an anonymous tip that alleged an elite team of US Army soldiers serving in Iraq had stolen a fortune in gold.

She would have blown off the mysterious lead if not for the list of six names and the date of the purported theft. Having been in that same area of Iraq at the time on a humanitarian story, she and Bill were each making discreet inquiries about the men implicated and she had tech support looking for a lead on the sender. Although she didn't care for anonymous tips, no matter how often they panned out, she knew people enjoyed the drama and adventure of being a faceless, nameless source blowing the whistle on some unpleasant situation.

What she'd die for about now was a tip for a juicy exposé on local spas. Surely she could find a way to pitch that idea. She'd happily volunteer as the guinea pig for any "undercover" research too. She could already hear the laughter from her team if she made such a suggestion. Her entire MO was leaving the fluff pieces and the half-baked ratings bait to the other guys. The guys who weren't winning awards the way her team did year after year.

She reminded herself that she had left Hollywood for many reasons, not the least of which was to find a place where substance mattered more than the smoke and innuendo of the next dramatic scandal.

By the time she slid into the backseat of the commuter car waiting for her at the curb, her phone had vibrated with another three alerts. Her determination to remain accessible to her team often conflicted with her goal of developing a worthwhile personal life. With a sigh, she retrieved her phone from her purse and checked the various alerts of email and two voice mail messages forwarded from the office.

In the first voice mail, she was pleasantly surprised to hear her father's voice. She'd called him days ago hoping he had a name or some insight on getting around the army bureaucracy she'd slammed up against as she tried to find confirmation on the names listed. Her dad, a legend in Hollywood, had produced and directed movies ranging from highbrow documentaries to summer blockbusters and seemed to have friends and contacts around the world in all branches of business. According to his brief message, he wasn't ready to call in a favor for her. His best advice was to work the story from the ground up.

As if she hadn't been doing that. Well, calling him had been a long shot.

The next voice message was from Parker Lawton, making yet another terse request to meet. She deleted it and shoved the phone back in her purse. Lawton was the last name on the list, and she wanted some solid facts and a better overall picture of the situation and the men involved before they had a conversation. She didn't want a possible thief skewing the perspective on the story.

It infuriated her when the subjects of budding stories learned her team was poking around. Most likely the anonymous tipster had let something slip, unable to keep from making a not-so-veiled threat or suggestion. As a producer, she had to assess the value and impact of a story before they had the facts. After several years on the job, her instincts were spot-on, and the repeated messages from Lawton confirmed her hunch that he had either something to confess or something to hide.

She and Bill had divided the list of names and created a cover story about soldiers returning to civilian life to explain their interest in the six men named by the source. Cautiously checking into Lawton's current situation had been Bill's job. So why was Lawton fixating on her? Her mind stirred it around and around, refusing to let go of work, even as she paid the car service and entered her apartment building in the heart of Russian Hill.

Inside, she locked the door behind her. She kicked off her work heels and dropped her purse on the nearest chair, fishing out her phone and taking it with her to the bedroom. Using the voice commands, she called Bill while she changed clothes for the evening. Her date was taking her to some elite awards gala. He'd been dropping the names of San Francisco's wealthiest and brightest innovators all week, to make sure she didn't back out. She didn't have the heart to tell him she'd already met the business rock stars on his list at one event or another.

"What are you doing calling me? You're supposed to be off the clock," Bill said in lieu of anything as mundane as *hello*. "You told me you were going on the date."

Reporters, she'd learned from day one, were a habitually nosy lot. "I'm dressing while we speak."

A low wolf whistle carried through the room. "Now, *that's* an image."

She laughed. He'd seen her at her best, her average and even her worst more than once when they traveled to remote locations in search of the story. Through it all, Bill had become a hybrid of friend and mentor with a side of big brother tossed in for good measure.

"You don't scare me." She laughed, knowing Bill was far more likely to be picturing her date. "What kind of dirt are you finding on Parker Lawton?"

"Why?" Bill asked, in a whisper. "What did he say?"

Interesting. Bill was a legend in the industry for maintaining his cool in every circumstance. Why was he nervous? "Nothing. The man has left messages for me all day that don't say anything other than he wants to meet in person. His emails are the same. Shouldn't he be calling you instead of me?"

Bill's sigh filtered through the speaker.

"His assistant was a brick wall when I reached out as myself," he said. "So I tried Lawton's personal number. I left him a message as your assistant, saying we wanted to interview him for his perspective on the sudden rise of homegrown terrorism."

Her hand stilled on the hanger supporting the little black dress she'd been pulling out of her closet. "That wasn't the story we agreed to."

"I know." He sounded miserable. "Since he's in the security business, it seemed more likely to get a response."

Though she might not care for the changeup, she couldn't fault his logic. "What else is going wrong with this story, Bill?" Warning bells were ringing in her mind, and that twitch between her shoulder blades was back. "I'm thinking we need to back off and reassess."

"Not yet. I know we're onto something important."

"Where are you right now?" She swiveled around and checked the clock by her bed. Maybe they could meet and tweak the plan before her date arrived.

"Some hole-in-the-wall diner off Pier 80 waiting on Theo Manning."

Pier 80 meant there was no chance she could get there and back, or convince her date to go by the area before the gala. "We confirmed he was the commanding officer of the team at the time, right?"

"Yes," Bill answered.

"And he's late?" Her intuition was humming. "That doesn't fit my image of a CO."

"He's a civilian now," Bill pointed out. "A crane operator. Late doesn't mean he's changed his mind about talking with me. A thousand things could have happened on the job."

"True." Propping her phone on the bathroom counter, she wriggled into the dress. "Tell me what you've found on Lawton while we wait." Bill might be a capable grown man, but she wasn't going to leave him sitting alone in a diner in a rough part of town until she absolutely had to end the call.

"Lawton's finances and net worth were a big surprise."

She unzipped her makeup bag and started adding shadow and eyeliner to go from office to gala-ready. "Is he destitute or filthy rich?"

"The latter," Bill said. "If your definition includes newly minted billionaires," he added in a low murmur.

Becca bobbled her mascara tube and it fell to the floor. "What?" Scrambling, she fished it out from under the counter with her toe as she kept talking. "Why did you hold on to that detail? Is private security that lucrative? Are the others rich too?"

"I didn't lead with that tidbit because I hadn't

finished my due diligence. Security might be that lucrative. His client list is privileged."

She snorted. "Not legally."

"Possibly legally. At any rate, I'm still trying to find out where and when he made his fortune."

Selling or hoarding Iraqi gold would certainly boost anyone's bottom line, though a net worth of billions seemed unlikely when the gold had been split between six thieves. Or so the source said. Huh. Maybe the source wasn't the victim as they'd inferred from the tip. Maybe their source was bitter about being cut out or shorted of his part of the fortune. "Send me what you have on Lawton right now and I'll help you sort it out."

"Your date won't appreciate you canceling at the last minute," he said.

"I'm not canceling," she promised.

"Oh?" Bill chuckled. "Even better. He'll love watching you google another man between bites of hors d'oeuvres."

She laughed with him. Better that than letting him know how close to the mark his teasing struck. "A personal life is essential to true happiness," she said. She'd written the reminder on a sticky note and kept it on her mirror where she could see it every morning. "Send it. I'll sort it out *after* my date. We can go over everything in the morning."

"Fine. I'll give Mr. Former CO another fifteen minutes and then I'm bailing. I'd rather give the Lawton tree another shake anyway. Maybe money will fall on my head."

"If he tries to bribe you, you'd better share."

Bill laughed again. "Not a chance," he said, and ended the call.

Bill was as effective and persistent as a bloodhound when he caught the scent of a story. Producing for him had taught her a great deal about how to piece together clues, unravel a background and identify the essential nature of what wasn't said in an interview. She liked to believe he'd benefitted from working with her as well. She enjoyed making sure her reporters came across with compassion as well as reliable authority for the audience. Unlike many of their competitors, they never broadcast a story until they knew they had the facts, and she used her specific skills to create a show that kept viewers coming back week after week.

They were definitely onto something with this gold theft story. She added highlighter strategically around her eyes and swept a shimmery powder just above her neckline while her mind sifted through the public records and recent articles on Lawton and his business.

They'd started the research file with the obvious

and easily accessible details on each of the names listed by the source. Last known addresses, employers, positive or negative publicity, etc. Returning to civilian life as a security expert wasn't a big stretch for Lawton, who'd served in the army for twelve years. A stash of stolen gold in his pocket would have made it easier to set up shop in the Bay Area, to be sure.

She poked through her makeup bag, seeking the perfect lipstick for the evening. Finding a tube of her favorite soft peach color, she slowly dragged it over her lips. Her mind drifted to Parker Lawton's publicity shot. His thick brown hair had plenty of waves, despite the short cut. The photographer had captured a savvy glint in those serious dark brown eyes. Considering his chiseled jawline, she figured if the man hadn't stolen any gold, he'd definitely stolen more than one heart along the way in his thirty-two years.

Her front door buzzer sounded and she capped the tube of lipstick, dropping it into her evening clutch. Time to make another attempt at refining the rather abstract concept of her personal life. Whether or not the evening went well, it was a plus to have a hot date to an A-list party. She'd even convinced herself she wasn't offended that her date had probably only asked her out in hopes that he'd get an inside track to her well-known father.

She opened the door without looking through the peephole and found herself face-to-face with the man she'd been daydreaming about—Parker Lawton, accused thief. For a moment she gawked at him. She decided the photographer had been a hack to only catch the glint in his eyes. The man's allure drew her in despite his casual khaki work pants, faded blue zippered sweatshirt and black ivy cap. In her heels, she was nearly eye level with him, and the intensity in his dark chocolate gaze muddled her thoughts.

"Pardon me—"

She pushed the door closed on his greeting and he stopped her, wedging his booted foot into the space. "You're *not* welcome here." She gritted her teeth and put all her weight into the effort of squishing his foot.

"Steel-toed," he said calmly. "Can't even feel it. I just want to talk."

"Not tonight. I'll call you tomorrow."

"Pardon my skepticism. You haven't returned any of my calls or emails. Can I have five minutes?"

"No." She shoved at the door again. "I'm on my way out."

"With this guy?"

He stuck a cell phone through the space and showed her a picture of her date at the elevator downstairs.

"What did you do?"

"Bought myself five minutes."

The stunt only confirmed that he was willing to fight dirty. "You have no right to be here." She leaned into the door again, despite the lack of progress. "How did you find me?" She had an unlisted number and the apartment was rented under the network's corporate account.

"It's what I do," he replied. "Look, I've heard someone is trying to cause trouble for me and some friends. Can you just confirm if you're working up a story on me and the men I served with in Iraq?"

Working up a story? Her temper caught like a match to paper. They dealt with facts, not fiction. "I'm a producer, not a reporter," she replied with the last thread of professionalism.

"Not buying the obtuse routine, red."

Red, ha. As if he was the first to try and get away with that nickname. She was far more than the hair and freckles, and many a man had learned that the hard way. "I'll be smarter tomorrow. At the office," she added, clipping each syllable.

He leaned into the door, making it clear he could force his way in at any moment. "Tell me who told you to look into my team."

"Never," she vowed. "That's Journalism 101, Mr. Lawton. I will not reveal a source."

"You're a producer, not a reporter."

"Still applies."

The elevator at the end of the hall chimed an arrival on her floor. "Guess your time's up, Mr. Lawton."

His boot was gone and without it the door snapped shut before she finished the sentence. She opened it again to find the hallway empty except for her date, striding forward with an eager smile.

Clutching her evening bag, Becca did her best to match his pleasant expression while she willed the heat of temper to fade from her cheeks. Her date chattered aimlessly as she locked her door and they walked down the hall. She slid her hand into his at the elevator, knowing Lawton had to be close. Telling herself it wasn't misplaced paranoia didn't change the sensation that the man was watching her. He knew where she lived and she didn't trust him not to try something else.

She clung to the fact that soon she'd be out of his view and his reach. No sane man would dare make a move while she was with her date and surrounded by people at the awards gala. And afterward? The idea of coming home alone sent a little shiver of trepidation down her spine.

Well, she'd cross that bridge when she reached it. For now, she would focus on her personal life. Beaming a high-wattage smile at her date, she set out to enjoy the evening.

Oh, that smile on her face irked Parker. He hadn't found anything during his recon of Rebecca Wallace, award-winning producer, that indicated a romantic attachment worthy of that heart-stopping dress and killer heels.

He waited until they were gone to move out of the alcove near the stairwell. He was an idiot for confronting her at her door. But he was getting desperate. The bizarre blackmail note had arrived yesterday, claiming media outlets had been notified last week, and granting him five days to make restitution for the gold he and his team stole from an Iraqi family or the men listed at the bottom of the single page would be killed one by one.

Theo Manning, Jeff Bruce, Franklin Toomey, Matt Donaldson and Ray Peters were more than soldiers. They were friends. The six of them shared a bond forged on several challenging assignments during Parker's last deployment. Together they'd handled a sensitive intel-gathering mission near the Iranian border. While it might have been easy to learn they'd all served in Iraq, it shouldn't have been as easy to connect them as part of the same team on that operation.

While they'd been deployed nearby and, through the course of the mission, had contact with the family listed as the victim, Parker and his team were innocent. None of them were thieves and he in particular had no cause to steal anything, not even back then.

He'd been ready to write off the note as a sick joke until a reporter called the office, asking for his opinion on soldiers successfully returning to civilian life. His assistant handled those comments on his behalf, as she usually did. While he was debating how to investigate the origin of the blackmail note, he'd received a call on his personal line about his opinion on locally grown terrorists. The timing was too close to be a coincidence. Someone had started snooping, and Parker needed to know who'd set them on this wild-goose chase.

Working the situation as he might do for a client, Parker scrambled to carefully reconnect with the men named in the blackmail note. He'd debated the wisdom of warning them about the note and the possibility of reporters and instead had suggested a guys' weekend. He hadn't seen the point in dredging up uncomfortable memories or causing worry over something that probably wouldn't amount to anything.

Then Theo had called back, saying he'd agreed to meet with Bill Gatlin, anchor reporter for one of the top special report shows. It was the red flag Parker couldn't ignore. He'd spent the day hustling up information on Gatlin, Wallace and the network. If other shows had the blackmailer's tip, it seemed Wallace's team had been the first to bite. And Theo's name had been the first on the list.

Parker had been given five days—four now—to return gold valued at over a million dollars. No exchange details or contact information had been provided, only an assurance that Parker would know where to bring either the gold or the equivalent in US currency when it was time. Logic and history said making the payoff was a tactical error, yet Parker planned to do whatever was necessary to keep those men alive.

Having been stonewalled by Wallace's gatekeepers at the network, he'd given up trying the polite approach. While he appreciated that they hadn't run the story on speculation and zero evidence, he didn't have time to play ethics games. He needed the name of the source or some clue he could follow so he could peel back the layers of anonymity and handle the jerk tossing around these outrageous, damaging allegations.

Parker lingered in the hallway, recalling his cursory searches of Rebecca Wallace and her reporter Bill Gatlin. At first glance, they were both workaholics and married to their jobs. He didn't know where the reporter was tonight, but he knew where Wallace was not.

He'd had his boot in her doorway long enough to learn her apartment security amounted to two dead bolts and a chain. Far easier for him to bypass the locks here than get past the systems protecting her office at the network building. He strolled up to her door, pulled his lock-picking kit from the thigh pocket of his work pants and was inside in less than a minute.

A quick survey of the space told him she was tidy, she spent little time here or she had an excellent cleaning service. He roamed around, appreciating the decor and furnishings. She went for classy and practical, not overdone or overpriced. As a business owner and a building owner, he knew the going rate for a two-bedroom apartment in this area and decided producing for a popular network show must pay well.

The master bedroom felt more lived-in. Though the bed was neatly made and the closet well organized, the various notes she'd left for herself here and there, along with the overflowing laundry hamper, gave him a sense of her as a more accessible person. He couldn't blame her for coming off as a prim snob during their tussle at the door.

The second bedroom she clearly used as a home office and guest room. He searched the desk, found an invitation to a gala that explained the little black dress, but no sign of the lead he needed. If she'd ever brought information on the bogus theft home, it wasn't here now. Leaving the room as he'd found it, he checked the more common and uncommon places people stashed important information. Nothing. She didn't even have a briefcase or a laptop here tonight.

On a sigh, he mentally adjusted his evening plans, knowing the next stop would need to be her office at the network. With his hands fisted in his jacket pockets, he was aimed for the front door when another idea struck. Returning to her bedroom, he found a tablet as well as an e-reader. "Yes!" he cheered softly when he opened the tablet and found her email applications were still open.

He searched through her inbox and the main folders, grumbling when he found all of his email messages moved to the trash folder. Were the days of professional courtesy gone? At least his assistant had handled the initial inquiry professionally while he was still waiting for Wallace to return his calls.

Continuing his search, he learned how she organized her files. He couldn't find a way to access any progress they were making on the story about him and his team, but he could tell it had nothing to do with soldiers returning to civilian life.

Sitting on the blue suede bench at the end of her bed, he searched through her email folders until he found an email from the previous week with Soldiers Steal Gold in the subject line. *Bingo.* The email was written in a similar tone to the blackmail note Parker received. While the author of the email didn't threaten anyone on the show, the names of those involved were the same, and listed in the same order as the note he had tucked into his wallet.

The allegations in the email were ghastly, making Parker's skin crawl. His team had worked their mission and followed orders. The implications—with no evidence to back them up—that he and the others were corrupt, brutal thieves infuriated him. The last few lines and the unique closing really caught his attention. The writer, pleading to maintain anonymity, thanked Rebecca and Bill for their kindness and integrity during their visit to the Iraqi village where the theft allegedly occurred. He—Parker was certain the writer was a man—gave the producer's ego another stroke by claiming Rebecca was the only person who could be trusted to handle this the right way.

The original email was bad enough, but the instructions she added when she forwarded the email to her reporter hit him like a sucker punch.

Bill, reach out to the family. Verify their safety and if/when the gold was stolen. If this is from Fadi, why would he insist on anonymity?

Parker swore. Fadi was a common name. In context with the other details laid out in the email, he couldn't dismiss the possibility that she was referring to the same young man they'd employed as a translator when they were in that area.

Did Rebecca know who'd sent the tip raising questions and spreading rumors about his team? The way he read and reread the email, she sure suspected the tip on the theft had come from the oldest son of the victimized family. No wonder she'd avoided Parker and refused to give up her source. Hell. He wouldn't get anywhere with her if she felt some misplaced obligation to cooperate with the person trying to discredit his team.

Well, he wasn't leaving empty-handed. He had a better idea of where the tip originated from, which gave him a better starting point than he'd had an hour ago. After his service in Iraq, he had people he could reach out to as well. He set her tablet back to the home screen and wiped off his fingerprints before slipping it back into the bedside drawer.

After locking her front door, he let himself out of her apartment through the fire escape and headed home to work the new lead. He needed to find the show with their report from that trip to Iraq and start fitting the pieces together. When he went to her office in the morning, he would insist on hearing everything about her trip to Iraq and why she was so eager to believe the worst of him and his team.

He stalked down the street, needing to walk off the anger simmering in his system. It wouldn't be smart to call for a car or catch a bus so close to her apartment. From his pocket, his phone rang. Seeing Theo's name and face on the screen, he picked up immediately.

"How did things go?" he asked. There was a long pause on the other end of the line and he heard several voices in the background. "Theo?"

"Mr. Lawton?"

Parker froze. This wasn't Theo. "Yes?"

"My apologies, sir. This is Detective Calvin Baird of the SFPD. I'm calling from Theo Manning's phone, as we've just opened an investigation."

A detective's involvement could mean any number of new problems and most likely the work of a busy blackmailer. "What kind of investigation?" He put his back to the wall of the nearest building and studied the action around him on the street.

The detective ignored the question. "According to his phone log, you spoke with him recently."

"That's true." Parker's stomach clutched and his pulse kicked into fight mode. "Where is Theo? Can I talk to him?"

"I'm sorry to say it, but he's dead," Baird replied.

No. Parker couldn't catch his breath. His hand gripped the phone hard and he slid down to land on his backside as the grief stunned him. He was on the phone with a homicide detective. What had happened to the five days the blackmailer had given him?

"Mr. Lawton?"

"Yeah." He swallowed the emotion choking him. "I'm here. What do you know? Where is he?" *Was.* Theo was gone. Parker cleared his throat. "How did it happen?"

"Nine-one-one received a call about shots fired about forty minutes ago. By the time the responding officers and paramedics arrived, it was too late. I am sorry for your loss."

"Was I the last to call him?"

"According to his phone log, you were one of two people trying to reach him."

"Who was the other?"

"I'm not ready to comment on that yet," Baird said. "I just arrived on the scene and we have very little to go on right now. Do you have time to come by the Bayview Police Station tomorrow morning? I should have more details for you by then."

Bayview? That hardly narrowed it down. The large district covered the port where Theo worked along with the southeastern part of the city. "Yes, of course." Parker knew the drill. If he wasn't a suspect, he was a person of interest. Unfortunately, his alibi was best not confirmed, since it involved his harassing a woman followed by breaking and entering.

"Thank you—"

"Hang on a second," Parker interrupted. "You mentioned gunshots. How did Theo die?"

"It's too soon for the coroner's report," the detective hedged.

Parker stood up, pulled himself together and applied the tone he'd once used to lead others in and out of harrowing conflicts. "He was my CO and a friend. What appears to be the cause of death, in your *opinion*?"

"Unofficially, sir, I'd blame the two bullets in the back of his head."

Parker's vision hazed red. Assassination less than twenty-four hours after he'd reached out to Theo. If the blackmailer thought *this* would motivate him to cooperate, to pay a debt he didn't owe, he was mistaken.

"Officers are canvassing the area for witnesses," Baird continued. "I'm hoping for a better picture of what happened by morning."

"No signs of a struggle?"

"Not at first glance, but we are in an alley."

Parker cringed at the image. "Thank you, Detective. I'll come by your office first thing in the morning." Tonight he had more work to do. He took another minute after the call ended to say a prayer for Theo. Real grieving required time he didn't have right now.

The blackmail note taunted him. Why ransom his team for gold they'd never stolen and then ignore the timeline? Something was off, and he intended to figure it out before anyone else on that list got hurt.

Chapter Two

The gala wasn't living up to Becca's hopes for the evening. Oh, the glitz and glamour made a visual impact, although her date clearly had an agenda. His conversation revolved around her father's work, and he hoped one day to work with him on a project. The scenario was familiar territory for Becca, who listened with only half an ear as he droned on. If he could pitch his big idea to her father and add a side trip under her skirt, his life would be complete. He didn't say that last part in so many words, of course. He let his wandering hands make his point clear.

She admired the timing and efficiency of the dinner and award presentations, but now, with only dancing, celebrating and mingling on the schedule, her mind kept circling back to Parker Lawton's shocking appearance at her door.

Did he often slum around dressed like a normal person rather than a new-money billionaire? She glanced across the room, trying to picture Rush Grayson, local billionaire and one of tonight's award winners, dressed as a typical workingman. Could happen, she supposed, squinting a little. She shook off the distraction. How Lawton dressed wasn't the point. He'd bullied his way into her personal space. She should report him, except the police would laugh her out of the station. Everyone presumed reporters resorted to similar tactics and worse when pursuing a story.

"I'm not sure I like the way you're staring at my husband."

With a start, Becca turned to see Rush's wife at her side, smiling and holding out a glass of champagne. "Oh! Hi, Lucy." Thank goodness it was a friend who understood Becca could appear more than a little fierce when she was concentrating. "Congratulations to Rush."

"I'll pass it along." Lucy was radiant in a strapless ice-blue gown, pride in her husband sparkling in her dark eyes. "Dare I ask who has your attention?"

"Don't worry. It's not a story. Well, it is, sort of." Becca clamped her lips together to cease the babbling. "I'm rattled."

"Never thought I'd see it," Lucy said, linking her arm with Becca's. "Do you need to walk it off?"

"Sure." The warm offer drained a bit of the tension dogging her since Lawton's appearance. "Some distance from Mr. Grab Hands wouldn't hurt."

Lucy's expression sobered. "Do you need an assist?"

"No. I have plenty of practice brushing off people who only want to meet Dad." She glanced over her shoulder to see her date occupied with the men they'd been seated with at dinner. Eventually, he'd notice she'd left and come racing after her with an inane compliment on his lips before he suggested a weekend in LA. "You'd think the red hair would make guys like that more wary of the reputed temper."

"The freckles undermine the effect," Lucy said, echoing Becca's theory. "Want me to get him tossed out? Rush and I can take you home."

"Not yet." Becca's gaze meandered as they walked from the ballroom to the mezzanine, where guests milled around between the open bar stations. She searched for a safer topic. "It seems married life agrees with both of you."

"It does," Lucy said. "I know people think I married him for the money, but the opposite is true. He married me for my common sense."

Becca chuckled. Although Lucy and Rush might not have had smooth sailing on their journey to wedded bliss, it was absolutely clear it was a love story.

"You know, most of the serious money in San

Francisco is represented right here and some of it is single," Lucy teased.

Most. By reputation or introduction, she knew many of the people in the room. She was well aware of who was loaded, who liked to flaunt it and who preferred flying under the radar. Until tonight, she'd had no idea Parker Lawton had a place among the financial elite. "Do you know Parker Lawton?"

"We've met a few times." Lucy's lips pursed. "Why do you ask?"

"Put away the matchmaker ideas," she said quickly. Some days Becca cursed her rampant curiosity, fostered by her father's habit of giving everything and everyone a fascinating backstory. Unwilling to explain how she'd first heard Lawton's name, she gave Lucy the cover story. "He's local and he's had such success after his military service," she said breezily. "Bill's been trying to get him to sit down for an interview."

"I expected Parker to be here tonight," Lucy said, her eyes traveling over the guests. "I would've been happy to introduce you."

That derailed Becca's wandering thoughts. "You did? Why?"

Lucy tipped her head toward her husband, pure happiness shining in her eyes. "Because Rush invited him."

For a moment Becca's mind reset the evening, inserting Lawton as her date, replacing tepid compliments with witty banter and a discovery of mutual interests. The man probably had a tuxedo tailored to his impressive physique. *Stop it*. His wardrobe wouldn't make any difference, she decided. If he'd been here, as her date or as a guest, he would have harangued her for the name of her source. *Still better than dodging Mr. Grab Hands all night*, a small voice in her head pointed out.

"How do they know each other?" Becca asked.

"Goes back to high school, I think," Lucy replied. "Although I didn't get the impression they were particularly close then. If you need a character endorsement, I'll go on the record that Parker's a stand-up guy."

"Huh." It seemed the safest response Becca could offer. Sticking a boot in her door wasn't a stand-up kind of move in her book, but Lucy didn't toss out character references willy-nilly.

"What's next for you at the network? I know you were eyeing a move up the ladder."

Becca mimed locking her lips and tossing away the key. "I'm happy where I am. Tell me what's next for you. Off the record."

Lucy's lips curved into a smile packed with barely leashed secrets. She drew Becca a few steps away from the nearest guests. "We're expecting," she said, eyes twinkling. She smoothed a palm over her trim waistline as her eyes darted around to make sure no one was watching them. "I'll be showing soon."

"That's wonderful," Becca said. "You must be thrilled."

"We're well beyond thrilled and floating somewhere in the galaxy of obnoxiously happy parents-to-be. I feel a little sorry for everyone who knows us."

Becca gave Lucy a heartfelt hug. "You'll be amazing parents. The rest of us will have to get used to a new, impossibly high standard." When she saw Lucy tearing up, she added, "I may just have to tip off one of the gossip sites."

As she'd hoped, her friend laughed out loud and the sheen of tears vanished. "You don't have such low friends."

"Of course I do," she protested. "I just keep them stashed in LA."

Lucy laughed again and, as Rush walked toward them, Becca promised to take her for a spa day soon.

Sipping the rest of her champagne, she made a game of staying out of her date's sight, making new friends as she worked her way around the room. She should just go home, though she wasn't ready to be alone and she didn't feel right about intruding on Lucy and Rush. Desperate for a distraction, she found a quieter spot and sent a text message to Bill, asking about the interview with Theo Manning.

Bill replied immediately, explaining Manning had been a no-show.

She should tell him about Lawton's visit and had her fingers poised to do just that when she changed her mind. He'd only insist she move in with him for a couple of days. Not happening. She'd be better off getting a room here at the hotel for the evening.

When Bill asked, she shared how well the evening was *not* going with Mr. Grab Hands. Welcoming the snarky replies, she was soon chuckling at herself for this latest failure at establishing a personal life. Her eyes landed on Rush and Lucy on the other side of the mezzanine and she sighed.

Love was lovely for them. Becca just wasn't cut out for the interpersonal stuff. She had her career to love. She had a stable of reporters who gave her plenty of ups and downs to juggle. She'd pit a moody reporter against the grumpiest toddler any day of the week. It might not look like a standard life, but it was hers.

Wishing Bill a good night, Becca went to find one more glass of champagne before going to the front desk to book a room. Better alone in a posh suite than home wondering when Lawton would come back and knock down her door.

At his place, Parker finished shaving and dressed for the gala. It seemed every breath was a new battle to keep his grief at bay. With a last check of his appearance, he decided it wouldn't get any better tonight. He grabbed the go-bag he kept ready in the coat closet, added another change of clothes and a rain jacket considering the season. Parker planned to be a much harder target for the assassin who had double-tapped Theo. Packing up his computer, he left his apartment, one eye searching for anyone too interested in the building or himself. He thought longingly of the SUV he'd had armored and knew it was too soon to reveal that asset.

Tossing the gear into the small space behind the driver's seat of his black-and-silver Audi R8 Spyder, he headed out, arriving at the awards gala well past the point of fashionably late. One perk was the lack of a wait at the valet stand. Easing out of the low-slung sports car, he tossed the keys to the valet. He flashed a fifty-dollar bill and pressed it into the young man's hand. "Keep it close. I may need a quick getaway," he said with a wink.

The kid grinned conspiratorially and promised Parker a zero wait time. Didn't matter. With the upgraded locking system, Parker could get into his car without the key he'd handed to the valet.

As he walked through the extravagant lobby, he scanned the attendees milling about on the mezzanine level. Resisting the urge to tug at his bow tie, he did his best to believe he looked like all the rest of the men in tuxedos. Although he preferred his military mess kit on formal occasions, tonight he needed to blend in with the upper echelons of San Francisco society.

He knew it wasn't wise to pester her again after she'd made it clear she'd speak with him tomorrow at her office. He just couldn't wait. A man was dead, cut down in his prime by a coward who'd ambushed him. Eyeing the free-flowing champagne, Parker hoped to have more luck this time. He deserved a chance to share his side of the bogus story, to counter every unsubstantiated claim in that email.

More important, he intended to make her understand that Theo should be allowed to rest in peace, free of any scandal casting shadows over his honorable service.

She would give him the name of her source by morning, and he would take that information to Detective Baird.

At the top of the wide staircase, he wandered left, bypassing the first two bars and the long lines of men and women in glittering formal wear. Reconnaissance was the first step in getting a handle on the situation and the woman. After two circuits of the areas designated for the event and the acquisition of a champagne flute he was using as a prop, he still hadn't found her.

She was here. He kept his gaze roving, eager for a flash of her auburn hair or those long, creamy legs. Striving for the patience he used to demonstrate in the field, he planted himself where he could watch the majority of the guests come and go.

At last he spotted her, walking up the stairs from the lobby alone. Where was her date? Her red hair gleamed, swept up off her neck in a sleek twist. The short black dress and sky-high heels with the sparkling straps winding around her ankles showed off her toned legs. At her door, in those heels, she'd been almost eye level with him. Her bright blue eyes, full of defiance and intelligence and amped up for the evening, had captivated him, putting an unexpected sizzle of attraction in his blood.

Forget that. He didn't need her to like him, and he'd blown any possible personal advantage by being a jerk earlier. Now he'd have to adjust his approach. He moved cautiously, using the crowd as cover to follow her when she reached the top of the stairs, so she wouldn't bolt. He wasn't in the mood to chase her around a hotel or out into the chilly October night.

He didn't want to tell her about Theo, didn't want to use his friend's death that way, but he was prepared to fight dirty and play the sympathy card if necessary. He couldn't afford to give the blackmailer any more of a head start.

How to get a stubborn woman to talk? He drifted after her as she aimed toward the ballroom where the dinner and presentations had been held. To save the rest of the men named as targets, he needed to succeed on his first attempt, not flounder around hoping for her cooperation.

His skills didn't run to charm, and with his heart in a vise over Theo, his patience was waning. The best option was to draw her away from the party, isolate her and make her see the wisdom of cooperating with him.

She tossed back her head, laughing at some flirty greeting from a man who appeared at her elbow offering champagne. Then she suddenly turned toward Parker, as if she'd sensed him staring.

Parker smiled, holding his ground while he waited for her to react. Her eyes went wide with recognition. From one second to the next, her initial shock shifted into a glare that would have split him in two if her eyes had been weapons. He merely raised his glass in a silent salute.

She turned away, returning her full attention to the people surrounding her.

He started toward her, taking his time, assessing the people around her as he practiced polite phrasing over and over in his head. She continued to check on his progress, something he found inappropriately satisfying under the circumstances. With growing confidence, he anticipated having her full attention, and the name of her source, before the night was over.

Fluttering her eyelashes at her entourage, she excused herself and moved toward the restrooms. Did she really think that would stop him?

Another man halted her, blocking her path just as she turned the corner. She stepped to the side and the stranger did the same, in that awkward dance of two people who were striving to be courteous.

Parker saw the danger a moment too late. The stranger's startled expression clouded over and he yanked Rebecca around the corner and out of sight. Hurrying through the crowded space, Parker wondered why she wasn't screaming. The woman had put up more resistance against him.

He turned into the corridor only to be blocked by a second man. Younger, trimmer than the first, he was moving into position to make sure no one interfered. *Not your day*, Parker thought. With two quick strikes, he disabled the sentry and pulled him out of sight of the partygoers.

He raced down the hall toward the stairwell, where Rebecca was struggling against the stranger's hold, fighting to stay on this side of the door.

Parker charged forward.

"Halt," the man ordered. "This is not your concern."

Parker skidded to a stop, trying to place the clipped accent. Still fighting, Rebecca glowered, pointing an accusing finger at him, her mouth opening and closing on words she couldn't get past her captor's throat-crushing arm.

"Let her go," Parker said, taking another step. The man pressed a syringe to her neck. Rebecca's body arched violently and then went limp. "No! Stop!" Parker shouted, advancing once more.

The man's mouth twisted into a nasty gap-toothed smile and as he wrestled Rebecca's body into the stairwell, Parker saw a pale scar bisecting his cheek from lip to temple.

Parker leaped into action again. The stranger couldn't have her, not when she was Parker's best chance to identify the person trying to blackmail him and discredit his team. He plowed through the door and straight at them.

Startled, the man shoved Rebecca's limp body at

him and raced up the stairs. Parker eased her to the floor and pressed his fingers to her neck. Finding a pulse, he started after her assailant, only to hear the fire alarms go off. He didn't believe for a second that there was a fire, but he was the only person who had good cause to doubt the alarm.

If he left her there, the accomplice could grab her or she might be injured by people fleeing the building with the false alarm. Scooping her up and over his shoulder, he hurried down the stairs, as voices of frightened people heeding the alarms and emergency lights filled the stairwell.

Knowing he couldn't wait at the valet stand with an unconscious woman over his shoulder, he headed for the parking area. "Come on, kid, where'd you put my baby?" Pressing the panic button on the extra fob in his pocket, he waited for the response. When the lights flashed and the horn sounded, he hurried over to the Spyder and punched his code into the panel on the door.

Settling her into the seat and fastening the safety belt, he checked her pulse again before closing the passenger door and sliding into the driver's seat. The engine rumbled at the press of the start button and he maneuvered out of the parking area before it clogged with staff and guests escaping the hotel.

"Just a producer, huh?" Parker snorted as he followed the path of least traffic resistance away from the hotel. "Someone wants you as badly as I do."

This latest unexpected development bothered him. Was the goal chaos or was there a logical end game? All of his training warned him he was dealing with two opponents with different agendas, yet it seemed quite a coincidence that they would attack at the same time.

What he needed was more information from her and about her. He wouldn't get the first until she woke up. There was no telling how long that would take, or if she'd be cooperative when she did. If he could find a safe place for her to sleep off the drug, he could use the time to dig deeper into her past for a possible kidnapping motive.

At the next opportunity, Parker shifted his route to head west. There was a property with an ocean view that he kept as a rental under the company name, complete with a safe room. Initially he'd planned to live there and he'd handled every detail of the security measures as an exercise to see what could be done more than because he feared a home invasion or an attack.

The rental, currently empty, would be their safest bet. He drove around for half an hour until he was sure he wasn't being followed. When he carried Rebecca inside, he took her straight to the safe room and tucked her in on the love seat, covering her with a cashmere throw.

He removed her high heels and cleared the safe room of items she might use against him. He removed any tech that could be used to communicate with the outside world. He didn't want her giving away their position to his—or her—enemies.

With a little luck, in a few hours she'd wake up and they could have a calm conversation without any extra ears or distractions. Armed with information, they could go their separate ways and never have to speak to each other again.

Chapter Three

Becca came awake slowly, her eyes gritty and her throat dry as she tried to get her bearings. The lights were dim and she had the immediate impression of being in a pleasant small sitting room. Someone had removed her shoes, tucked her in and covered her with an incredibly soft throw. The gesture left her wary rather than comforted. What happened?

Easing herself upright, she found herself on a love seat upholstered in deep burgundy leather so smooth it felt like silk to the touch. Not Bill's house. She didn't recognize the space, couldn't name a single friend who had a room like this. Where were her shoes?

"Hello?" Her throat was dry enough that she sounded like a frog. How long had she been here? She called out a couple more times, receiving no answer.

Fear trickled down her spine, a chill under her

skin that burned as questions burst through her clouded mind. Where was she? Who brought her here? *Why?*

She stood up and the room turned in a sick, lopsided circle. Falling back, she let the love seat catch her as she tried to force herself to remember something. Anything. A bottle of water had been placed on the end table between the love seat and chair. Terribly thirsty, she reached for it and then snatched her hand back. The bottle looked new, but that was no guarantee it was safe to drink.

"Think," she whispered to herself. Someone had put her here, and she had no intention of making it easy for them to keep her. She fingered the hem of her dress, vaguely recalling her boredom with her date. They'd been at a hotel. A party. Snippets of the evening floated in a disjointed parade through her brain. A grand staircase, free-flowing champagne and beautiful people twisted in a kaleidoscope that made her eyes ache and her head pound.

When she felt steadier she stood up again. Doing a slow three-sixty, she took in the rest of the room. The space was cleverly designed in a narrow rectangle with a refrigerator, microwave, small oven and sink making up a kitchenette at one end. On the opposite end of the long room was a single door and next to that a set of floor-to-ceiling doors. She walked closer and found a Murphy bed.

"I've been kidnapped by a tiny house architect," she said aloud, imagining Bill's laughter and snarky retort.

This was more luxurious than some of the movie trailers she'd seen while working on sets with her dad. She bounced a little, discovering the floor didn't have any give the way a trailer floor often did. Another tremor slipped over her skin. A trailer could be moved anywhere, at any time. Who would do this?

There were no windows, only a lovely painting of the Golden Gate Bridge spearing out of a thick fog bank. All of the lighting came from LED fixtures in the ceiling. What she assumed was the entrance door was painted the same warm ivory as the rest of the walls, but with the oversize hinges and cross-bars, it looked more like a bank vault. She walked over, pushing and tugging at the spoked handle. Her grip was weak; her entire body felt used up and she couldn't make the wheel budge in any direction.

A flat panel on the side of the door lit up and a feminine computerized voice announced, "The status of the safe room is secure."

"Good to know." Becca tapped the panel, and a command screen appeared. Not seeing an icon or a button to unlock the door, she spoke clearly in the direction of the speaker above the panel. "Unlock safe room."

After a moment, the computer denied her request.

"Thanks for nothing," Becca muttered. She walked the length of the room, looking for a switch to make the lights brighter. Apparently that too was controlled by a system outside her reach. Not even the reading lamp on the end table tucked between the love seat and the oversize tufted leather armchair responded when she flipped the switch. "Where am I?"

More silence. Apparently not even the computer had an answer.

She went to the kitchen sink and tested the water faucet. The water smelled fine and looked clear. The cool water on her hands refreshed her and she blotted her face as well before finding a cup and drinking her fill.

Her memories returned in fractured images. She remembered walking with Lucy, but not what they talked about. There had been a strong man holding her tightly. He'd smelled funny. Odd. Too sweet and strong for a cologne, the odor had made her head swim. Chloroform? Was she recalling fact or was her mind weaving in some fiction?

Uncertain, she crossed to the other end of the room, opening the bathroom door, finding no windows and no obvious escape route. A glance in the mirror had her scrubbing away the mascara smudged and streaked under her eyes and down her cheeks. Noticing a red mark at her neck, she rubbed at the spot, remembering the pinch and sting of a needle before her world went black. Someone had shouted. Who had it been?

"Where am I?" she asked, returning to the center of the room.

"You're in a safe room."

She jumped. This reply was not automated. The voice, as rough as sandpaper thanks to one of those altering devices, filled the room. "Cooperate, Ms. Wallace, and you will be released unharmed."

She heard the unspoken flip side of the statement. If she didn't cooperate she wouldn't be released. "Come in here and say that," she said with all the bravado she could muster. "Show yourself!" Her temper mounted as she waited for a reply. "You coward! It will take more than voice alteration and an automatic door to avoid the penalty for kidnapping me." She needed to keep him talking, needed information about her captor.

"We'll see."

Male, she was sure of that much. Ninety percent sure, anyway. Those voice gadgets could do bizarre things. "Let me out!

"People will be looking for me." She hoped they already were.

There was another long delay before the reply. "Rest. Drink plenty of fluids. We'll talk again soon."

"What do you want from me?"

"For now, I want you to rest."

"Where are my shoes?" She shouted the question at the door and pulled on the handle again. Her frustration soaring to new highs, she smacked the control panel, hoping for a short circuit if nothing else.

"Escape is impossible without the code and my palm print."

She swore at the door and the electronic panel that was currently dark. "Unlock this door."

"As soon as it's safe, I will."

"When this door opens I'll—"

"I understand your distress. You will not be harmed in my care."

Becca shivered. Something about the voice, the cadence of it, felt both familiar and frightening. "I won't make the same promise to you."

"The basics are stocked for you," the gravelly, distorted voice said. "Meals will be provided three times each day."

When left to her own devices, she didn't eat three regular meals each day. "What makes you think I'll eat?" A hunger strike might be her fastest way out of this room.

"Eating is your choice," the voice replied. "But I will not allow you to harm yourself."

"Oh, that's your job, huh?" She crossed her arms to hide her trembling hands. "What do you want? Money?" Had one of her notoriously bad dates gone off the rails in an effort to get her father's attention? "Name your price." She'd gladly give up the password to her untouched trust fund account in exchange for the code to leave this well-appointed prison.

"No," the voice said. "Cooperate and this will be over soon."

Cooperate with a faceless kidnapper? No way. "Buddy, this won't be over until I'm free and you're locked up in a prison cell," she shouted at the ceiling.

The speaker crackled once and went silent. The vault-like door remained closed. Knowing the effort was futile, she walked to the panel and poked at it again anyway.

One dead end did not a hopeless situation make, she told herself, not quite believing it. She couldn't bring to mind any situation quite as bad as this one.

Her father's film company had been detained once in Turkey. It had been a miserable and uncertain forty-eight hours under house arrest, before all the paperwork was considered acceptable to the authorities and they were allowed to leave.

As stressful as that had been, this was worse. Here, she was alone, trapped by someone who had yet to make any real demands. She felt her molars grinding on the tension and forced herself to take a few calming breaths.

She'd survived worse things than this. Turkey had been dangerous. Working the story with Bill in Iraq, right on the Iranian border, had been a huge risk. Anymore, dating was akin to Russian roulette. No way was she going out of this life in the role of a helpless captive.

"What do you want from me?" she shouted at the door.

The silence built and built until she ended it with a loud, long scream worthy of the worst horror flick. Cutting loose, she released all her bottled-up fury into the sound, imagining her captor's ears bleeding from the assault.

He might be in control for now, but there had to be something here she could use against him. Her dad had gone through a horror flick phase and she'd learned a great deal about improvised weapons on those sets. Not to mention all the time she'd spent with prop masters, learning how to fashion amazingly realistic things with little more than duct tape and a good idea.

Her captor had been smart enough to confiscate her high heels. No matter. That was only the first, and most obvious, option. She reviewed the small room through a new lens, with the primary goal of escape.

The love seat wouldn't be much help, unless it had a pullout option. It didn't. She examined every inch of the shelves and the items they held. The CD cases could be sharpened with a little effort.

For at least the tenth time since she'd woken up, she reached for her cell phone and felt that swell of panic when she didn't find it. How pathetic to be so dependent on a device no bigger than an index card. She'd noticed that her captor had also stripped the space of any technology that could be used to communicate with the outside world. Not even a remote for the television remained.

That meant careful planning and forethought. Was all this for her specifically, or just because she was unlucky girl number whatever? She battled back another surge of fear and blinked away the tears threatening to turn into a pitiful sob. She would not let this bastard watch her cry.

Having noticed two surveillance cameras, she retreated to the bathroom, which was the only place he couldn't keep an eye on her. Maybe no cameras in the bathroom qualified him as a decent sort among the kidnapper set, but it did little to improve her opinion of him.

PARKER WATCHED THE woman carefully through the two cameras he'd installed in the room, feeling better now that she was moving around so well. Fighting back was another good sign.

The drug hadn't kept her down long, thankfully. In the two hours he'd watched her sleeping off the effects, he hadn't come up with an acceptable explanation to offer if he had to take her to an emergency room. The only friend with medical training he trusted in a situation as sticky as this one lived in Nevada, and also happened to be the third man on the blackmailer's list.

Her blatant search for something to use as a weapon left him smiling. She didn't give a damn that her captor knew what she was up to. Grit and courage were traits he admired. He shook off the sensation. He didn't want to admire anything about Rebecca Wallace. She was a means to an end and he should stop wasting time coddling her.

If she was strong enough to argue with him and fight with the locked door, she was strong enough to tell him her source. His finger hovered over the communication link before he pulled it back. As soon as he demanded answers, she'd know it was him keeping her locked away. What would he do with the information at half past one in the morning anyway? Better to wait, to learn more about her. He'd prefer to find a way to handle this without exposing himself to a lawsuit or criminal charges.

It was a relief when she ducked into the bathroom and out of his sight, ending his one-sided debate.

There was no way for her to escape. She'd accept that soon enough. Fortunately for him, there wasn't anyone else to hear her screaming, though he hoped she didn't do that again any time soon. The woman had excellent projection and stamina. Rubbing his aching ears, he returned to his search into her background, looking for anything that made her a target.

He glanced up at the monitor when she emerged from the bathroom. She'd let her hair down and he'd bet the clip was tucked in her bra or somewhere she thought to use it as a weapon. Fair enough. When she brushed a finger under her nose, he zoomed in on her face and cursed himself. She'd been crying. In the one place where she knew he couldn't watch.

What had he done here? After a few hours, he was already dangerously close to feeling guilty about locking her in the safe room, even if it was for her protection. Guilt didn't suit him. He assessed and took action according to mission parameters. That philosophy had served him well in the field and equally well in his civilian endeavors. It would serve him well as he tracked down the blackmailer.

Parker pulled the tie from his tuxedo collar, wrapping and unwrapping the length of fabric around his knuckles. He'd mined her school records from high school through college. She'd made straight A's through a tough course load peppered with every form of drama club and literature classes. According to her first résumé out of college, she'd held lead roles in some of the stage productions. He supposed that went along with being the daughter of a powerful force in Hollywood. Those details trickled down and eventually disappeared as she applied for jobs that took her away from Southern California. She'd had an interesting journey to her current post as a producer.

Nothing in the first layers of her background pointed to motive for kidnapping. His mind followed the logic back to his first theory that the scarred man's attempt to take her was connected to the blackmailer and the source feeding the media lies about Parker's team. It wasn't the least bit uplifting.

Satisfied she was alert and out of immediate danger, he felt better about leaving her unattended while he made the quick trip over to her place. She wouldn't be comfortable in that dress indefinitely. Hopefully a gesture of goodwill in the form of clean clothes would be a step in overcoming her justified anger.

With a sigh, he synced the app that would let him keep an eye on her and this condo through his phone. As he changed clothes, he decided the only silver lining was that she didn't seem to remember he'd been around when the scarred man grabbed her. He didn't expect that to last much longer.

BECCA PACED THE length of the room, considering her options. In the bathroom, she'd taken the clip from her hair and broken it in two pieces. One was inside her bra, the other tucked into her garter. She wanted to be prepared if her captor came in and tried something. As weapons, the pieces wouldn't cause much damage, but they might buy her a few precious seconds to get away.

She loosened the zipper on her dress, wishing she could take it off. Although the little black dress was considered a wardrobe staple, perfect for every occasion, she was ready to be done with it. What she wouldn't give for yoga pants and her threadbare college sweatshirt. And some thick socks. Her sheer stockings did nothing to protect her feet from the cold tiled floor.

It was a peculiar experience for her to not know the time. Her entire life revolved around her daily routine. Good grief, she wanted to know the *day*. Was anyone looking for her yet? Had a ransom been issued? Would her captor be demanding payment from the network or her family? She supposed that depended on the reason for taking her captive. If the goal was money, he'd be better off dealing with her directly. She could just imagine her dad ignoring a critical voice mail or email because he had a movie to finish or business to handle.

Tears threatened once more. He'd always been tough, though she knew he loved her. They loved each other. The gap had just become too wide after her mother died. Flattened by his grief, he'd never quite made it back to really connect with her. They hadn't had a real conversation in months, and that last one hadn't been uplifting for either of them. She hoped that terse exchange wouldn't be their last.

Her stomach rumbled and she decided to make use of the basics her captor had stocked. Finding peanut butter in the cabinet and bread in the refrigerator, she used a spoon and made a sandwich. "Good thing I don't have a peanut allergy," she said, raising the sandwich to the camera. "Did you check my medical records?" She poured another glass of water from the tap, not ready to trust the chilled bottles.

She ate standing up, refusing to be caught at a disadvantage. "It really is a good use of space," she said, in case her captor was listening. "Efficient too. Must have cost you a fortune with the design, the build and all the security measures."

Security. The word ricocheted through her brain. Parker Lawton handled security for high-end clients like the Gray Box data storage solution company co-founded by Rush Grayson. Could he be foolish enough to hold her hostage? It wasn't outside the realm of possibility. He had been dumb enough to stick a boot in her door and demand information.

Much as she tried, she couldn't recall seeing him at the party. Of course that didn't mean he hadn't been there, only that her memory was still recovering from whatever drug had knocked her out. If—*when*—she got out of here, if Lawton was the captor behind the speakers and cameras, she would make sure gold theft was the least of the charges against him.

With renewed resolve, she returned to the bathroom and closed the door. This was a safe room per the computer and her captor, making it a safe bet that the room was inside a building. If she could loosen a pipe or somehow cause a leak, that would draw someone's attention. At the very least, her captor would need to come in and repair it, giving her an opening to escape.

She knelt down to peer under the sink, and the lights went out. Biting back a startled scream, she scrambled to her feet and reached for the door handle. It locked under her hand. She was trapped in the dark, half expecting some monster to lunge out of the shower stall, when the deep, altered voice carried through the closed door.

"Time to talk, Ms. Wallace." He was in the safe room, having made his move when he knew she couldn't attack.

She pounded on the door. "Lawton, is that you?"

"No."

It had to be. "Prove it." She hammered another fist on the door. "Let me out."

"In good time. I need some information."

She clapped a hand over her mouth to smother the weak plea that nearly promised him anything in exchange for her freedom. Becca Wallace did not beg.

"If you cooperate—"

"Oh, stop with the threats and get to the point," she snapped, somehow keeping her voice steady.

"Your show has a good reputation."

What? She bit back a sharp retort. Maybe it was her awful date. Surely Lawton was smart enough to know he couldn't win her over with ridiculous, mild compliments. "Good? We win awards, thank you very much."

"How do you decide on ideas for the show?"

The question threw her off. Lawton or the dumb date? "I can assure you we don't let kidnappers dictate our topics."

"Walk me through it," he insisted.

She decided to play along. It was the only way to get clues about her captor. Turning slightly into the door, she tried to imagine the person on the other side. "My reporters usually pitch the ideas. We discuss them in meetings, looking for a fresh angle on newsworthy events."

"How much time to get from idea to broadcast?"

"It varies." Although the device altered his voice, she could tell the sound was originating from a point a few inches above her. More potential proof she was dealing with a man, since she was only a couple inches under six feet tall herself.

Her mind reviewed the men she could remember from the gala, starting with her date and Lawton when he'd been at her apartment door. Her date had been a smidge shorter than Lawton.

"Ms. Wallace?"

"What?" Lost in thought, she hadn't heard the question.

"I asked you how the show handles anonymous tips."

Her opinion swung back to pinning this on Lawton, though if she called him out, he'd only deny it. She had to give him enough rope to hang himself. "Depends on whether the tip is legitimate."

Practicing the same diligence they used on a story, she mentally flipped through the topics and features of their recent broadcasts. One of those had started anonymously, over six months ago. The research and legwork on that one had been grueling, but she'd refused to take the easy and obvious route simply for the sensation factor and ratings. The segment had aired last week with a fresh, objective perspective on a hot-button issue regarding energy costs.

"Is this some convoluted attempt to pitch me a show?" she asked.

"No."

The single word held a sharp edge that had her easing back from the door. Although he'd been polite so far, she had the sense that pushing him too hard and too soon would be a big mistake.

"How do you determine the validity of an anonymous tip?" he said in that same edgy tone.

"I'm not going to reveal my sources," she stated. "You can accept that right now." What if something for an upcoming show had leaked or one of her reporters had rattled the wrong cage? She had to confirm who she was dealing with, and fast.

"Isn't that a protection limited to reporters?" he asked.

"You know we could swing by a court and ask a judge," she suggested. Through the door she heard him sigh. She gave herself a point on her imaginary scoreboard. "What? Aren't you ready to accept the consequences of kidnapping me?"

"Tell me what happens when you get an anonymous tip for a story," he demanded.

"If the story is interesting, we spend long days tracking down confirmations of the allegations. We have plenty of days banging our heads against walls, stalled out when people won't talk to us. Invariably we spend a ridiculous amount of time speculating and hoping for a break. Anonymous sources can be big time and energy drains while we search. Most of the time we ignore them," she finished, hoping he'd believe it.

"If you don't get the break?"

"Without confirmation, my show doesn't tell the story. It sits in a potential idea file until additional and indisputable information comes through."

"Sounds like a strange way to run a news program."

She bristled. "You're a producer now as well as a kidnapping scumbag? Haven't you seen the show? For your information, we deliver content designed to engage and enlighten our audience. My team doesn't chase the daily or weekly news cycle. We choose to delve deep into the issues that matter, the situations—good and bad—that have a lasting impact on our community as a whole."

Silence was the only answer to her outburst. She was getting tired of him going mute. Long minutes of silence combined with the dark surrounding her made her sympathize with claustrophobics. Was he still out there? She pressed her ear to the seam of the door. Only more of that empty silence, not even the sound of his breathing. Maybe he'd left and was just being a jerk about the lights. She twisted the door handle, swearing to find it remained locked. As she'd given him a piece of her mind, he made his complete control of the situation, and of her, crystal clear.

"Let me out of here!" She pounded her fists against the door. "I will flood this room," she threatened.

"You can't," he replied. "I control the water supply."

Of course he did. The idea made her mad and she clung to the anger rather than admit to even a shred of relief that he was still in the safe room with her. "Let me go. You're making a huge mistake. People will be looking for me. Let me go and I won't press charges."

"Have you ever been wrong, Ms. Wallace?"

The question, asked so calmly, interrupted the chaotic cycle of despair and fear. "Yes." She'd been wrong to go to the gala, for starters.

"Have you ever been wrong about a story?" he pressed.

There were too many ways to answer that question, and she refused to have him twist her words around. For all she knew, he was recording this conversation to use against her and the network. "I stand by the finished product of every broadcast," she replied.

"Do you ever identify the anonymous sources?"

Almost always, usually by the process of elimination or when the person had a change of heart. "Sometimes."

"Before or after you run the story?"

This was Lawton. Had to be. She tried to take comfort in the fact that with Lawton as her captor she wasn't at the mercy of a psychopath or pervert or a flat-out madman. Only a thief bent on hiding the truth. Money and power did strange things to people. Even respected, stand-up-guy kinds of people.

"Ms. Wallace?"

"Rebecca," she said. According to the psych classes she took in college, a first name established a more personal bond. Anything for him to see her as a person rather than a useful tool.

"Rebecca." Her name, altered by the device and muffled by the door, sounded so strange. Goose bumps raced along her skin and she was grateful he couldn't see her hands shaking.

"Before or after the story?" he asked again.

"Rarely before the story airs," she admitted. "Some sources are better at disguising themselves." It was so obvious he wanted to know who'd sent the tip about the gold theft. She had her suspicions, but no proof. Just as she suspected it was Lawton on the other side of this door and couldn't yet prove it.

"In what way?"

Would he never give up? "Very few people can resist their fifteen minutes of fame. Aside from that, the bigger the story is, the more options there are for the source. Usually, though, with sensitive information, only a few people have access and we can figure it out, if only by process of elimination. I prefer…" She didn't finish the sentence as her temper flared to life again. She preferred a normal interview style. She preferred having civilized conversations.

"You prefer what?"

"My preference is to have all of our sources sign a statement with the network, under the agreement that we will never expose them. In my opinion, that choice gives them more credibility."

"Thank you."

"Does that mean I'm free to go?"

"In due time," he said. "I've done all I can to make your stay pleasant. You'll find a meal in the kitchen. Feel free to make use of the Murphy bed."

"Wait. I don't want to stay." She gripped the door handle in both hands and tugged mightily, willing it to move. "Wait!" she cried again. "I won't tell anyone about this," she pleaded. "Please, let me go."

He didn't answer. A moment later the computerized voice announced the safe room was secure.

"Yippee." The bathroom door was still locked. She dropped her forehead to the door and debated the pros and cons of crying again. Would he see that as a ploy or a weakness?

Before she could decide if she had any tears left to cry, the lock clicked and the door opened when she turned the handle. She stepped out into the room and found herself alone. The homey aroma of pancakes and bacon wafted through the space. Was it really morning, or was he messing with her idea of time? She forgot the food when she saw the small black suitcase in front of the love seat. She reminded herself that although it looked familiar, most black suitcases did.

Becca walked over and flipped the tag and felt another spike of fear. The luggage tag sporting the network logo was hers. And on the other side of the handle she found the white daisy sticker she applied to make her black suitcase stand out from all the others.

Her brain slid into a panicked loop that she was in more trouble than she realized. It didn't matter if it was Lawton or someone else. Her captor had too much access. He'd not only been to her apartment, he'd been *through* it. He'd gone into her closet and found her suitcase and presumably packed it with her belongings. As if being held against her will wasn't enough of a violation.

Becca backed up and sat down in the chair, as far from the suitcase as she could get without returning to the bathroom. She didn't want anything he'd touched. The little black dress would do just fine for now. Forever, she added, glaring at the suitcase. And that was a dumb idea. If she cooperated, maybe he would relax his protocols. She had to make him think he was winning.

Resisting the sensation of complete helplessness, she finally unzipped her suitcase. He'd been careful here too, as if he knew how a woman's mind worked when she was cornered. He wanted to make her stay pleasant? Well, she didn't have any intention of *staying* a moment longer than necessary.

There were jeans, T-shirts, pajamas, bras and panties, socks, tennis shoes and a zip-up sweatshirt. Her travel bag of toiletries and makeup was tucked in place as well. He'd touched it all. While she was grateful to have her own things, she couldn't shake the feeling it was all tainted by the man who'd rooted through her home, her most private and personal spaces. She rubbed the chill from her arms. This situation was unpleasant, not impossible. He'd promised not to hurt her. She hadn't made the same pledge.

Shifting to block the view of the camera perched in the corner near the door, she quickly opened the pocket of her suitcase where she kept a multitool stashed. Since she always had to leave the one in her purse at home when traveling, she'd purchased an extra and kept it in her suitcase. The pocket where she stowed it was empty. He'd thought of everything.

She sat back on her heels, reluctant to admit defeat. "I'll find a way out," she whispered to herself. "I am strong and smart." Her voice cracked on the affirmation, so she repeated it until she believed it.

Chapter Four

At precisely eight o'clock Friday morning, Parker turned in his room key at the front desk and walked out of the midpriced motel in the Mission District. He hadn't slept more than an hour in the last twenty-four, and he was running on adrenaline and strong coffee.

Couldn't be helped.

Until he had a handle on this situation, he wouldn't go home again or stay more than one night in the same place. Likewise he didn't want to bring attention to Rebecca's location by staying too long at that property. Before he'd left the motel room, he'd checked the app to confirm she was still well at the safe room. He'd spent the last hour answering emails for her so no one at her office would ask questions too soon.

With the strap of his duffel slung across his chest

and a worn briefcase in the old army digital camouflage pattern packed with Rebecca's cell phone and tablet as well as his devices, he stood at the valet stand and waited for his ride.

He owned three cars and stored them in various locations around town. Hours ago, he'd called in a favor and moved the Spyder away from prying eyes to the safety of Sam Bellemere's garage. The cofounder of Gray Box owned an entire building and had devoted one parking level to his car collection. Though driving on his own would be more convenient, Parker didn't want to make things too easy for whoever had set this mess into motion.

When the driver arrived, Parker climbed in and gave the address for the Gray Box offices. He figured it was the safest place in town to stow the personal belongings without undue questions. Then it would be time to meet Detective Baird at the Bayview station to discuss any progress on Theo's murder.

"I'll only be a minute or two," he said when the driver pulled to a stop in front of the building. He handed over the fare and a hefty tip. "Wait for me?"

"Yes, sir."

True to his word, Parker returned to the car without the bags within five minutes. His friend Rush Grayson, founder and namesake of Gray Box, had no problem stowing the gear for any length of time.

Aside from the men Parker had served with, Rush and Sam were the only people Parker counted as friends and trusted implicitly. The pair had been instrumental in helping Parker manage a surprise windfall inheritance while Parker had been serving overseas and they'd worked on several projects together since Parker opened his security firm.

Armed only with his phone, Parker used the security app to check on Rebecca again. Switching up the camera access, he checked the street outside the building as well for any signs of trouble. Thankfully, everything remained clear for now.

For a man known for making reliable, intelligent choices even in the heat of a gunfight, he kept doing everything wrong this time. Rebecca wasn't afraid of him. She hadn't called him by name yet, though he had to be at the top of her suspect list. If he'd been thinking clearly, he would have walked into the safe room and asked her outright about her source and her plans for the gold theft story. Then, assuming she hadn't attacked him, he could have persuaded her to stay in the safe room and out of danger while he went after the culprit.

Sorrow and lack of sleep weren't good enough reasons for his flawed decisions. Saving her from the real kidnapper last night was fine, but until he identified the man and the threat, he could hardly use that moment as evidence of cause and sound reasoning for keeping her locked up.

At the Bayview Police Station, he thanked the driver and tipped generously again. Logically, he knew life's scorecard rarely balanced, and even if it did, Parker knew it would take far more than a couple big tips to offset holding Rebecca Wallace against her will.

He pushed back against a fresh wave of guilt as he walked into the station to speak with the homicide detective who'd caught Theo's case.

Detective Calvin Baird was tall and lean, with ebony skin and close-cropped hair going gray at the temples. He shook hands with a firm economy of motion and encouraged Parker to have a seat in the chair by his desk.

"How are you holding up?" Baird asked.

"Theo was a good friend of mine," Parker began. "We served together in Iraq," he added. "Both of us grew up in and around San Francisco, but we didn't meet until the army introduced us."

"Small world," Baird said, nodding. "We have a fairly clear picture of what happened last night. No suspects so far. I assure you we will be digging deeper, interviewing witnesses and such. I'm sorry you lost a friend."

"Me too." Parker sat forward. "What do you know?"

"According to his coworkers, he planned to meet someone at a diner a few blocks from Pier 80. His shift ran late and he decided to walk it. After that, it appears someone came up behind him, shot him twice in the back of the head and pushed or dragged his body into the alley."

"Theo never had a chance?" That didn't make any sense.

"That's how it looks right now. We're still processing evidence and creating a timeline."

Parker could see the question in his eyes. "I wasn't anywhere close to that neighborhood yesterday." He pulled out his phone and sent a text to the office. "I'll have the office send over my itinerary so you can corroborate."

"I didn't ask," Baird pointed out.

Parker shrugged. "Gotta cross the *t*'s and dot the *i*'s, right?"

"Right." Baird leaned back. "Were you aware he was on his way to meet with a reporter at that diner?"

"No," Parker replied. "Was the reporter the other phone number on Theo's call history?"

Baird nodded slowly, his dark gaze inscrutable.

"No idea who called nine-one-one?" Parker asked.

"None," Baird replied. "When SFPD arrived, your friend was alone and deceased."

Parker struggled to stay seated and calm. He felt

as if he could punch through cinder block about now. "He deserved a better exit from this world."

"Most of us do," Baird said. "The reporter came in when I called him earlier this morning. He didn't volunteer much about the interview topic, but he did help us with the timeline."

Parker hid his surprise over the reporter's cooperation. "Are you thinking the interview made Theo a target?"

"Anything is possible." Baird tapped his fingertips on the file. "The deviation in his routine might simply have put Mr. Manning in the wrong place at the wrong time. It's a rough neighborhood. I'm afraid it's too early to tell, unless you care to shed some light on why they were talking."

"Could be anything, I suppose." Parker propped his ankle on his opposite knee, deciding on the best way through this prickly situation. "I'm ashamed to say Theo and I hadn't seen each other recently. Didn't stay in touch as much as we should have. Overseas, we were tight. Had to be. Once we were home, we drifted apart."

"It's natural," the detective interjected, the weight of experience in his voice.

"It is." Parker met Baird's steady gaze and realized the detective really did understand. "How long did you serve?"

"Ten years in the navy," Baird said, sitting up straighter. "Another ten in navy reserves."

Parker relaxed a bit. "Doesn't make me feel any better for only reaching out to Theo a few times a year. I don't really know enough about his day-to-day life to give you a good picture of him. He didn't have any enemies during our service. Everyone liked him. Can't imagine that changed in the civilian sector. He was a good man."

Killing Theo made no sense. Why strike down anyone on the list before the ransom deadline? Whoever was pulling the strings had to know that wouldn't make Parker eager to cooperate. He had three days left to figure it out.

"I'm hearing the same. We will work this step-by-step," Baird promised. "I'm good at my job, Mr. Lawton, and I close cases. Someone has the information we need. If you think of anything else, give me a call." He handed Parker a business card.

"You got it."

Parker didn't bother pointing out Theo had been trained in enough forms of combat from hand-to-hand to rocket-propelled grenades that he might as well have been labeled a walking weapon. Baird would know that with one look at Theo's service record. The killer who'd managed to shoot him in the back of the head must have known that as well. A swift, silent surprise attack had been the best chance for success.

"Has next of kin been notified?" Parker asked.

Again, Baird consulted his notes. "His brother is on the way from Arizona. I expect the body will be released soon."

"Will you pass on my number?"

"Of course," Baird assured him.

With a handshake, Parker left the police station, the muscles in his jaw tight with frustration. Outside, he checked the app, confirmed Rebecca's status and put his mind back on his own investigation. There had to be a point where the bogus gold theft story, the blackmail note, Theo's killer and Rebecca's kidnapper intersected.

Using public transit this time, he crossed town to the network building and asked to speak with Rebecca. When they gave him the out-of-office message and expected return date he'd sent on her behalf through her email, he left his name and number and went on to Gray Box to pick up the gear he'd dropped off.

Rush, noticing his return, invited him upstairs for a quick word.

"Everything okay?" Rush asked when they walked into his office. "I noticed you were late to the gala and left without saying hello last night. Coffee?"

"Please." Parker stifled an oath. Hopefully Rush was the only one who noticed. "Congratulations," he said. "Sorry I missed your speech."

Rush laughed. "You've heard one acceptance, you've heard 'em all." He handed Parker a mug of black coffee and sat down on the long, modern couch in front of the windows that offered a stunning view of the city. "What kept you?"

Knowing that the closer the lie was to the truth, the easier it was for the liar, Parker sat down and told him about Theo. "They called me from the scene, since my number showed up in his recent call history. It shook me up."

"Sorry, man. Are you all right?"

"Not really." Parker shook his head and dropped his gaze to his boots, startled by the sudden wave of emotion threatening to pull him under. He had to keep his cool or be faced with increasingly uncomfortable questions. "Theo was one of the good guys, you know? I'm sad I won't talk to him again and I'm pissed off that he survived a few war zones only to get shot in a stateside alley."

Wisely, Rush only nodded his agreement. It hadn't been that long ago that Rush was up to his eyeballs in unfair and dangerous circumstances. He'd called Parker to dig up dirt on his wife's former employer, who turned out to be wanted for war crimes. The man had given Lucy a terrible ultimatum: steal information from a secure cloud account at Gray Box or her sister and nephew would die. Although Parker trusted Rush and his partner, Sam, he couldn't drag them into the mess he'd made.

"You know Sam and I would do anything for you, Parker?" Rush waited until he had his full attention. "Without you, we might not even be here."

Parker wasn't here for praise. Yes, he'd lent his expertise to both Rush and Sam recently. He'd handled the building security and assisted in a couple of sticky situations. Without the sage financial advice of Rush and Sam, Parker wouldn't be independently wealthy today. Unbidden, a small voice in his head wondered if being an average guy might have prevented this situation.

No sense leaping down that rabbit hole. Better to play the cards he'd been dealt than waste time and energy on the what-ifs. The money had been a blessing, empowering him to change his life as well as the lives of those he employed. He couldn't allow one coward wanting a chunk out of his bottom line to spoil his outlook. He had to stay locked on to who he was, not how he was viewed—a lesson he'd learned on his military operations.

Deciding to make use of the time Rush had given

him, Parker changed the subject. "What do you know about Rebecca Wallace?"

Rush's eyebrows arched in surprise. "Looking for an introduction?"

What was it about marriage that turned perfectly sane men turn into matchmakers? He dismissed the notion of playing along. "That's not what this is." She wouldn't have him anyway once she figured out he was the man holding her hostage. Why did that awareness annoy him? "The detective on Theo's case told me he was killed on the way to his meeting with one of the top reporters on the show she produces."

"All right." Rush frowned as if choosing his words carefully. "She's smart as a whip. Born and raised in the movie business in LA. Seemed to cause a stir when she moved up here, out of her father's shadow."

"You like her?"

"And I respect her," Rush said. "She knows the value of ratings, but she and her reporters get the facts straight. You were overseas when her show first featured Gray Box. She did another segment when we moved to this building. In both interviews her reporters asked tough questions and the end result was candid and overall positive publicity."

Parker didn't take the endorsement lightly. Rush and Sam, with their checkered pasts, hadn't always been treated fairly by the press. Now Rush and the company were big enough to effectively control any issues that might become problematic. It helped that his friends ran a clean business and maintained a product that remained impervious to computer hackers.

"Did you go to her?"

"No." Rush sipped his coffee. "Her reporters came to me."

"Why?"

"Why?" Rush echoed the question, clearly startled. "Sam and I were news. Our start-up made a splash, had huge success, and now we're investing in the community."

Parker hated lying to Rush after everything they'd been through. "I can't think of anything newsworthy going on in Theo's life."

"You could ask her," Rush pointed out. "I can make a call and get you into the office."

Parker shook his head. "Thanks anyway. I've called. She's out of the office. Her reporter hedged with the cops. He won't be any more open with me."

"No ideas why your friend was meeting with her reporter?"

Parker shook his head again, staring into the dark coffee in his mug.

"But you're going to look," Rush said.

"Wouldn't you?"

"I have. You remember what happened when the gossip columns declared Sam married to a woman I didn't know. Lucy and I went over immediately armed with champagne and doughnuts."

"And you called me." Parker had been armed with deadly weapons when Rush asked him to help keep an eye on the newlyweds.

"Turns out it was the right call." Rush leaned forward. "We weren't soldiers, but we have skills and resources. Connections, too. If you need us, Parker, *ask*."

He knew Rush, in business mode, was renowned for his savvy, his sound strategy and his ability to apply the right amount of pressure to a decision moment. It had been a long time since Parker felt someone could see through his defenses. "It's personal," he admitted.

Rush waited him out.

"Or it's a random crime and nothing at all," he added after another minute of internal warfare.

Rush leaned back and stretched his arms across the back of the couch as if he had all day for Parker to choose between opening up and walking out.

"I have it under control," he said, standing up. "Thanks for the coffee, the ear and the insight on Wallace. If there's a point when I'm in over my head,

I'll let you know." He hoped it wasn't obvious how close he was to sinking right now.

"You're the most capable man I know." Rush stood up and extended his hand. "But seriously, anything you need, just name it."

"There is one thing." Parker weighed the pros and cons of doing some of his work here. He didn't want his problems to blow back on Gray Box. It was no secret they contracted with his firm, so spending time here shouldn't raise any eyebrows. "Do you have a computer I could use to do some investigating—off the grid?"

Rush grinned with pride. "You know you're in the right place."

Parker followed Rush downstairs to an available cube on the cyber security level, just around the corner from Sam's high-tech and intimidating work space. He started his search by scouring Rebecca's cloud storage files for notes from the trip to Iraq. No anonymous sources on that story. She and Bill had gone looking for success stories between the US military and Iraqi communities and found several to use in their feature.

Her notes were peppered with locations, names, anecdotes and pictures, and once more he felt admiration and respect for her. Not for her, for her approach, he reminded himself. She and Bill had gone out of their way, two people and their crew on a morale-building tour that seemed to have positive effects. Knowing he had to get a hot meal over to her in the safe room, he transferred the rest of the Iraq files to a thumb drive for later review. If there was an overlap, it would surely be there.

When he skimmed through the broadcast history of the show, he noticed the way she balanced hard-hitting pieces with more upbeat, feel-good stories. He discovered Rebecca was just as Rush had described her. Tough, fair and thorough on the job, she let her reporters go for the jugular, but only after they'd done the research to prove the legitimacy of their approach.

He skimmed background notes on stories that were initiated with vague anonymous claims and confirmed she'd answered him honestly about how they proceeded and verified the facts in those situations.

Although he was glad to learn she hadn't lied, he wasn't happy that Theo died, likely caught in the cross fire of the typical verification process. Reading through her emails with Bill about the gold theft tip, he saw that between the two of them, they had tracked down current addresses and phone numbers on all the men listed.

Parker thought about asking Sam to look for any

evidence of a hacker monitoring her email and decided against it. He couldn't abuse the friendship by asking Sam or Rush to get actively involved, just in case she did manage to drag him into court over kidnapping her.

Someone wanted the gold theft story out there, and someone, other than him, was willing to kill to be sure it wasn't told. He forced himself to look at the situation strategically, turning it over to view it from all sides as he'd done during his military days. It was possible the source had used Rebecca to flush out Parker and his team and take them out. The theory left a bad taste in his mouth and left him wondering if the blackmail note was designed to accomplish the same thing. Neither theory explained going after Rebecca.

Taking advantage of working in an area where the signal couldn't be picked up by any outside surveillance, Parker picked his way through her cell phone apps and records for a look at her life and habits. Her life seemed to revolve entirely around her work. Aside from her trips to the grocery store and gym, there were only a few calendar entries that might qualify as dates. Even her social occasions were driven by network or community events like the awards gala last night.

This wasn't his first time evaluating a target.

Gathering and assessing intel and habits, despite the obvious privacy violations, created a better picture and revealed potential weak spots. Still, when he sat back and rolled the tension out of his shoulders, he wanted a shower to scour away the sensation that he'd been digging too deeply into her personal space.

"First time for everything," he said under his breath.

He blamed the bulk of his discomfort on the guilt of yanking her out of her life. Who was he kidding? The guilt was bubbling up because every time he peeled back a layer, he actually *liked* the woman more and, as Rush had said, he respected her work. She didn't allow her personal bias or that of her reporters into any of the finished broadcasts, though it cropped up in the planning stages.

Shutting down her tablet and phone, he packed up and forced himself to consider how to release her. He didn't want to let her go immediately. The risks were still too high. Yet he couldn't keep her locked in the safe room indefinitely, ignorant of why she was there, even if *he* thought it was the best place for her. Without undeniable proof that keeping her out of sight was best, he didn't stand a chance.

Outside, waiting on another rideshare driver, Parker checked on Rebecca once more. She wore faded jeans and a pale T-shirt and her feet were bare. Tucked into the armchair, she was munching on a meal bar. She had a pad of paper balanced on her up-drawn knees, and the pencil in her hand flew across the page, her head tilted to the side. For a moment, he did a double take, then recalled it had been in one of the pockets of her suitcase. He supposed a television producer raised in the movie business would have learned how to draw if only for storyboards or blocking sets, or to fulfill any number of new terms he'd learned since poking through her life. Curious, he made a mental note to check camera angles, in case she left the pad open.

When the driver arrived, he gave the address for another generic midpriced motel near the airport. Once there, he booked a room for the night under a fake name and credit card and stowed his belongings. Armed only with his cell phone and a 9mm pistol at his back, he called a cab for the ride to the west side of town, grabbed a burger and milk shake and walked to the condo where Rebecca was hidden.

He used the cameras to verify her position in the safe room and then shut off the lights, plunging the room into darkness. A moment later, he hit the microphone and used the voice alteration effect to order her into the bathroom.

"No."

He took his finger off the mic and sighed. He was too tired to fight with her. "Cooperate, Rebecca," he said, trying again.

She held her ground, standing in the middle of the room, hands on her hips, a defiant glint in her eye. Since he'd last checked on her, she'd pulled up her hair in a messy ponytail. "This has gone on long enough," she said. "People are looking for me, Lawton. Let me out."

So she knew. Or was willing to try and convince her captor that she knew his name. What was he thinking? He *was* her captor. He thought of the man with the scar who'd tried to take her. The memory put a bite into his voice when he said, "No one is looking for you." No one she wanted to find her, at any rate. "Into the bathroom."

"On one condition," she said.

"You're not in a position to negotiate."

"Don't lock me in this time. Please," she said, staring up at the camera near the door.

"Fine." He caught the flash of a triumphant smile before she turned and hurried to the bathroom. Her mind was working overtime on some angle.

When she reached the bathroom, he opened the safe room door only enough to slide the food through. Then he closed it and locked it, even as she ran across the room. He brought the lights up and turned off his mic.

"Yes!" She did a fist pump and picked up the burger and milk shake. "Thanks," she said, tossing another look at the camera before returning to the armchair with her food. "Is it lunchtime?"

He didn't reconnect the mic, just watched her happily devour her burger.

"No Q&A today, Lawton? What day is it?"

He stayed at the condo longer than he'd meant to, listening to the questions she hurled toward the ceiling while he studied her carefully. The woman was definitely up to something. He smiled, surprised how much he anticipated their next meeting.

BECCA SENSED HE was done talking to her. She suspected he might even be gone already, but she kept up a one-sided conversation just in case. He hadn't denied it when she called him Lawton. Of course, he hadn't confirmed it either. *That* would have been too much to ask.

What he had confirmed, bringing her a burger topped with sautéed mushrooms, Swiss cheese and mayo with a side of fried pickles and a chocolate-cherry milk shake was that he'd been poking through her life. Once a week, she splurged and ordered this lunch through an online app from her favorite family-owned burger joint near the office.

She wanted that to mean she was being kept near the office, and knew better than to jump to that conclusion. It was safe to assume from the hot burger and thick, cold shake that she was still in San Francisco.

"Consider this another offer to buy my way out of here. You have learned by now that I'm loaded, right?" As a new billionaire, Lawton wouldn't care about money. "I hope you didn't call Daddy. He's far too busy to bail out his daughter, even from a kidnapper."

She ate for a few minutes in silence, wondering what kind of conversational bait to dangle next. She wanted to keep him talking. Not because she was bored or lonely. That would be the definition of pathetic. No, she wanted him to talk so she could worm under his defenses and get out of here.

"Hey, Lawton, did I mention that I called him when I got stonewalled by the army?" She twirled her straw through the milk shake, grinning at the silly noise. "He has all kinds of friends in strange places. I thought he could help me get a more comprehensive look at your service record." She popped a pickle into her mouth, enjoying the tangy flavor.

"Don't worry, your secrets are safe. He didn't help. Dad doesn't believe in favors or handouts."

Not for daughters who flew the nest anyway.

"Are you even there?" she asked, peering at the camera again. At the continued silence, she polished off the burger, cleaned up her trash and returned to the chair.

Picking up the notepad again, she flipped over a new page and started drawing, letting her thoughts wander aimlessly. When she paused to stretch her hand, she realized she'd filled the page with sketches of Lawton.

The first was a detailed picture of his face when he'd been at her door, the ivy cap pushed back from it. Another one was a recreation of his head shot from his security firm's website. She'd drawn how she imagined he would look in a tuxedo. No, wait. That wasn't a guess; that was how she'd seen him at the gala. She picked up the pencil again, scrambling to get the images on the page as they flooded back into her mind.

As she sat back again, several faces stared back at her from the notepad. The happy expressions of Rush and Lucy, a man she didn't know with hard eyes and sharp features, and another man with a scarred cheek. But the face she couldn't look away from was Lawton's. She'd sketched him with eyes wide, lips parted and worry stamped on his forehead. He seemed to be pleading with someone. Could he have been begging her to drop the story?

She knew it was a memory. Now she just had to figure out what it meant and where it fit in with her previous recollections of the gala.

Chapter Five

Leaving the condo, Parker walked for several blocks, stopping here and there along the way and doubling back at one point to confirm he wasn't followed. Satisfied, he moved forward with his plan to pick up the SUV registered in his name. With luck, Theo's killer had eyes on the car and picking it up would draw out Parker's enemy. He couldn't develop an effective strategy or counterattack until he knew if he was up against one man, two or a team.

There had been two men at the hotel. He just didn't know if the sentry was a local hire or into this as deeply as the man with the scar. In Parker's experience, that snarl and the delight in his mean eyes when he'd put that syringe to Rebecca's neck added up to a man who enjoyed his work.

Feeling comfortable and confident behind the wheel of his own car, Parker had watched his mirrors for any sign of a tail as he cruised through the city, eventually reaching the pier where Theo had been a crane operator. He had two and a half days left to unravel this mess, and he didn't want to lose any other friends along the way.

He'd come down to ask questions about Theo's last days, hoping one of his coworkers would give him a new lead to work with. No one had seen Theo chatting with strangers. None of his friends on the job thought he'd been behaving strangely or show-ing signs of stress. Everything had been situation normal for Theo until he'd been shot.

Parker walked from the pier toward the diner, dar-ing either fate or the killer to take a shot at him. It was an idiot move, especially if Theo had been in the wrong place at the wrong time and a victim of local crime rather than the blackmailer. Passing by the alley again on his way back to the pier, he paused and stared at the fresh bloodstain about ten feet from the sidewalk.

It was too easy to picture Theo dead before he hit the pavement. The man had crossed the world going from one mission to the next, always willing to get in the trenches and get dirty and always eager to con-tribute to get the job done.

No one took a shot at Parker. No one spoke to him, though there were people milling about across the street and on the corner. He decided to leave the witnesses to the professionals and stalked toward the pier.

Returning to his SUV, he watched the cargo ships and port crews work while he gave the recent events consideration. He rolled his windows down, hoping the breeze off the bay would blow out the clouds of guilt and doubt muddling his thoughts. His instincts screamed *Danger*, yet he couldn't pinpoint the source. America had enemies and the army had enemies. Good grief, Parker had enemies. Not Theo. He'd been little more than a pawn on a global chessboard.

Whether or not Rebecca's reporter admitted it, he'd contacted Theo because of that anonymous tip. This couldn't have been a coincidence of local crime. Parker wasn't confined by the laws and was therefore free to make the logical leap. Bill had wanted information on the gold theft, or more likely the details of the mission around the time the gold was allegedly stolen. If the police got those pieces out of Bill, what would happen next?

Danger. Parker could practically smell it on the air.

At least Rebecca was safely out of the office and out of the scarred man's reach. Parker should probably encourage Bill to get out of town, but with the police active on the case, the reporter had a thin layer of protection in place. Parker had the sense that if the person pulling the strings on this wanted Bill dead, he'd be dead already.

He tapped his fingers absently on the door panel as he watched a crane operator load containers to the deck of a cargo ship, maneuvering each piece like another layer in a slow-moving, complex block-stacking game.

Yesterday, it had been Theo sitting in that crane. He'd told Parker how much he enjoyed working a job challenging enough and noisy enough to mute the ghosts from their combat years.

Parker swore. They lived in the same city and saw each other only a few times a year. Benign neglect was a lousy definition of friendship. They'd been through hell together and Theo had died worried that those nightmares had come calling for them.

He curled his fingers into tight fists and drummed them against the steering wheel. He wanted a target, needed a viable outlet for the rage building inside him.

His phone rang and seeing the Nevada area code and Jeff Bruce's face on the screen, he felt dread settle like a cold lump in his gut as he picked up. "Hello?"

"Parker?" The soft, feminine voice was thick with tears.

"Yes?"

"It's Naomi, Jeff's wife. He's…"

Her voice trailed off and Parker checked the phone to be sure the call hadn't dropped. "Naomi? What happened?" he asked, his pulse pounding in his ears. *Don't say dead, don't say dead.* Parker had made those calls to loved ones, and he wouldn't wish the experience on anyone. "Take a breath. Just take your time."

He heard her suck in a ragged breath and exhale slowly. "He's been in an accident," she said. "I'm at the hospital."

"I'm on my way." He started a mental list that began with unlocking the safe room door remotely and letting Rebecca know where to pick up the belongings he'd taken.

"No." Naomi sniffled. "I mean, that's not why I called. He said don't come."

What? "Okay." Why wouldn't Jeff want him out there?

"The police said his car was run off the road. Hit and run near a bridge. Between the seat belt and airbag he survived it. Another car stopped to help. They got him out before the river took his car." More sniffles. "The doctors are sure he'll recover."

"That's good news." His pulse returned to something closer to normal. "What do you need? How can

I help?" Parker had to get his head out of the sand and give clear warnings to everyone on the list. Keeping the ransom note to himself hadn't helped any of them. With two men on the list attacked, in order, he couldn't pretend the incidents were unrelated. His team deserved the heads-up, and being vigilant while separating theory from fact wouldn't hurt any of them. Hell, it might save what was left of them.

"He's back in surgery right now, but he said to tell you—only you—he saw the driver of the other car. He said it was Fadi."

Parker bit back the visceral protest. Jeff had to be wrong. Parker absolutely could not reconcile the smart, helpful young man they'd known with this cowardly act of attempted murder. "He was sure?"

"He was." She sniffled. "You know who he's talking about, who he saw, don't you?"

"Yes." He struggled to believe it. It had to be true; Jeff wasn't prone to hallucinations. "I promise I'll handle it," Parker assured her, having no idea how to keep that promise.

"When he got home after that deployment, Jeff talked about Fadi and the family frequently," she said. "He said he was one of the best locals he'd met over there. I got the impression any one of you would have vouched for him or his family. If he got his visa and made it over here, wouldn't he have reached out?"

"Yeah, you'd think so." Parker closed his eyes, but it was no defense against the onslaught of memories from those months of recon and analysis and careful interpretation of words and actions. "Are you going to be okay?"

"I'm upset," Naomi said. "Don't worry. I can pull myself together before he gets out of surgery."

"Let me know when he's out. I'd like to talk to him when he's ready."

Naomi promised to keep him updated and when the call ended, Parker sat there, dumbfounded. He felt as if he was mired in quicksand and every move he made dragged him closer to drowning.

At this point, with Theo dead and Jeff in the hospital, Parker had to assume the blackmail note was as bogus as the anonymous tip sent to Rebecca. It seemed like a safe bet they'd been contacted in order to flush out the entire team.

Although the kid was the obvious common denominator, Parker wasn't ready to take that bait. The Fadi Parker remembered had a clear head. Loyal and proud of his heritage, and aware of the political and geographical economics of the area, he wouldn't have been easily swayed by propaganda that would turn him against the Americans.

What on earth was he up against?

He needed to get back to his computer and dig into the thumb drive with the rest of Rebecca's notes from her trip to Iraq. He had to find the exact points where his mission and her visit overlapped and hope the answer gave him a worthwhile clue. Otherwise he was just spitting into the wind while someone picked off his friends.

BECCA WAS GOING stir-crazy in this room. She knew exactly how many steps she needed between the wall and the door, having counted it out a dozen times. Or more. By the same method she knew the distance in steps from the counter that served as a kitchen to the Murphy bed. Sure, the safe room was all tricked out, complete with the best of everything except a window or a clock. The indulgent decor choices didn't take the sting out of being held against her will.

There was an entertainment system, but the television and radio components had been removed, probably because the devices had been able to connect to the outside world.

"This is cruel and unusual punishment," she'd hollered at the camera near the door. "I can't even stream shows or movies." No, she was left with a small library of books and music CDs for amusement. Unfortunately for Parker Lawton, her mind needed more stimulation.

She'd spent what she considered the remainder of yesterday focused on the gala, sketching out every scene she could recall from the time she'd left the apartment with her less-than-stellar date to the moment she'd woken up in the safe room. By the time the third meal of fried chicken salad arrived, she'd been pretty confident in the order of events.

Not too hungry, after thinking it all through, she'd picked at the salad and stashed the rest in the refrigerator. Bored and frustrated, she gave up on a novel and applied her brainpower to finding a way out of this box. She hadn't come up with a good idea before she fell asleep.

Based on the eggs and toast that had been delivered while she was in the shower, she wanted to assume it was a new day. She detested this sense of helplessness, this utter lack of control as she wandered aimlessly from hour to hour without the anchor of her normal schedule.

When would Lawton let her go?

After the burger and milk shake exchange, she'd given up all pretenses that her captor could be anyone other than him. Who else lived in San Francisco, had virtually unlimited funds at his disposal and a reason to keep her out of his business? Those facts and the questions he asked were more than enough to convince her.

She debated the wisdom of causing damage to the safe room she'd likely have to live with and making him offers he couldn't refuse.

"This won't work, you know," she said, aiming her words at the entertainment system where the speakers pushed that deep, altered voice into the small space. "The network has to know by now that something's wrong. I don't take time off without significant planning. Someone will raise the alarm."

Hopefully someone already had. What was the minimum time before the police would take a missing-person report on an independent adult? "Bring a clock with the food next time," she muttered. "It's common decency."

On a wave of uncertainty, she took a long drink from her water glass. Just to change things up, she forced herself to consider the possibility that her kidnapper wasn't Parker Lawton.

There had been someone else at the gala. Sitting down, she flipped back through the pages in the notepad and studied the face with the scar that she'd sketched. What if *he* was her captor? She shivered, remembering the way his forearm had crushed her neck, nearly suffocating her.

What if that man was working for Lawton and

she'd been taken as leverage to drop the story about the stolen gold? Oh, good grief, playing the what-if game was as pointless as yet another rundown of the facts. What she needed was a distraction.

No, she needed to get out of here. Not just for her safety, but for her sanity.

She sat up and reached for her water glass, and the lights went out. Startled, she bumped the plastic tumbler with her hand and she heard the water splash onto the table and tile. "Lights! Please?"

"Remain seated," he ordered in that altered voice that scraped her nerves raw.

Once more she obeyed, despite her urge to leap into action. What good would it do when he could obviously see her with the cameras and she couldn't see anything other than layers of darkness?

She heard the lock disengage and the door open on a soft whoosh. Just as quickly, the door closed and locked again. His footsteps were barely audible as he approached.

"This really isn't fair," she protested, shifting in her seat.

Strong hands gripped her shoulders from over the back of the couch, pushing her deeper into the cushions. "Do not move."

She didn't think his hands felt as rough or heavy as those of the man with the scar, but she couldn't be completely sure. "Do I get an early release if I co-operate?" She hoped keeping it light would mitigate the strange mix of excitement and fear his presence stirred up in her.

"No."

"Then why bother?" She slid down and rolled off the love seat and out of his reach. Gaining her feet, she bolted for the door. Maybe while he was inside with her, there was a way to—

He was on her in the next instant, faster than a heartbeat, one of his arms clamped against her waist and a hot palm covering her mouth.

His chest created an unyielding wall at her back. She shifted her hips, seeking an advantage, and only managed to create an intimate contact better suited for a different kind of darkness.

"Screaming does nothing, remember?" The words, spoken at her ear, reverberated through her. It wasn't solely an effect of the voice alteration. The stubble on his jaw had scrubbed lightly across her skin with each word.

Slowly, he peeled his hand from her mouth.

She didn't embarrass herself by calling for help. Nothing had come of her one and only bloodcurdling scream, and nothing had come of any of her shouting matches that followed. When she tried again to pull away and gain some breathing room, he caught her wrists and pulled them behind her back. A moment later she felt the cool pinch of plastic, heard the rasp as zip ties were pulled snug against her skin.

"Wait a second," she protested. "You don't need to do this."

"It's done." One large hand circled her upper arm and he guided her unerringly around the furniture until she was seated in the armchair. "Now we're going to talk."

The touch branded her skin under his palm, leaving her chilled everywhere else. "No, please. Not like this." This prickly sensation under her skin had to be a rant brewing inside her. It was temper and frustration, not *attraction* to the man holding her hostage. Obviously she needed fresh air to clear away the cobwebs of being locked in here. "Please. Just cut me loose and I'll tell you whatever you want to hear."

"You don't leave until I say so," he said.

The digitized voice would have terrified her if she hadn't been so sure this was Lawton. Lucy wouldn't call him a stand-up guy if he was a complete jerk all the time. "Listen, Lawton, this is a big mistake. We all make them." She flexed her wrists, trying to get the zip ties to bite into her skin for proof later. "Restraining me only makes you look worse."

"Stop fidgeting." He leaned over the back of the chair. "You'll be released when I'm satisfied."

What did that mean? Was he suggesting she trade her body for her freedom? It sounded dreadful when he suggested it. Even though she was ninety-five percent sure this was Lawton, for the first time she was truly scared. It was one thing for her to make the offer, but to have him demand sex was completely different. She didn't care that it was a double standard.

"How many times have you been to Iraq?" he asked.

The question, so far outside her line of thinking, startled her. "Iraq? Once."

"And overseas?"

She clamped her lips together, ignoring her watery knees and the fear trickling down her spine with icy fingers. He'd been through her computer. If he wanted answers, he could untie her or go back and find out the hard way. She would not cooperate with him while he had her tied up.

"Why were you in Iraq?" He tugged on her bound wrists when she didn't reply. "Answer me, Rebecca."

"You already know." She tried to turn around, and he held her in place with one hand and his superior skills. "You can't keep this up. People will be looking for me by now."

"They aren't. Answer my questions and we'll both be out of here sooner."

No one was looking for her? He sounded too sure of himself. "What did you do?" she demanded.

"Give me a few answers and you'll be free to go find out for yourself."

Only more questions danced on her tongue. Questions, demands and promises of prosecution. She bit all of it back, swallowed it down. When she was free, she would be sure he paid the price for every inconvenience and worry he caused her.

"Why don't you work in Hollywood anymore?"

She wasn't fooled by the changeup. "It's none of your business."

"You should be glad I disagree with you." His hands stroked across her shoulders, in toward her neck and back out again, miraculously smoothing the tension out of her muscles. "Why?"

What was he up to now? Did he want to be her counselor or her massage therapist? She might as well play along until she had a better opening to escape. "Nepotism is an epidemic in Hollywood. No way to make my work stand on its own merit."

"Is your work that good?"

"Yes. My reporters are the best and we deliver a quality show. We were in Iraq because our teamwork is that good," she added. According to the source, the last village on their circuit had been attacked by insurgents the week after they left and the gold stolen by the Americans sent to clear out the intruders. "Did our presence put those people in jeopardy?"

"No."

The word rasped across her senses, a harsh counterpoint to the easy movements of his hands. "Tell me what happened during your tour," he said. "Tell me who you met, what you saw."

She gave in. What would holding back accomplish at this point? He was completely in control here, and nothing she said would change the past. Everything he wanted to know was on her computer, and she suspected he'd helped himself to that already. A small cooperation *might* get her out of these zip ties and out of this room sooner rather than later.

"We were escorted the entire time by a security detail. We only visited areas that had been clear for three weeks or so," she continued as the tastes and smells and the surprising sights filled her mind. "You remember all of that too, don't you, Lawton?"

He lifted his hands away and she could still smell the fresh soap on his skin. "Go on," he said.

She did. "We had two weeks once we left Baghdad, and we made the most of it." She shared every detail from those days packed with movement, light, trepidation and joy. The highs and lows of the trip had been fresh in her mind since the anonymous email hit her inbox.

"Did you ever see a fortune in gold?" he asked.

"No," she admitted. "The families we met and villages we visited were quite modest."

"And were they happy to chat with Americans?"

She nodded. "Yes. War is ugly, but the people were grateful for the positive changes."

"I see." His fingers lightly brushed down her arms. Calloused and cool, his touch slid to a stop just above the bindings, resting lightly on the pulse points of her wrists.

"Please let me go. I've told you everything."

"Not yet." He leaned closer, his breath warm on her hair, and somehow he managed not to touch her anywhere else. "Before someone sent you that trumped-up email about stolen gold, have you ever had contact from anyone you met in Iraq?"

She tried to stand up, but he kept her in place. "You cowardly bastard! You've been through my email?"

"Among other things," he said easily. "Answer me. Have you had contact with anyone from Iraq?"

She thought of Fadi. He'd been such an asset, helping them as a translator and sharing his remarkable culture with her, Bill and their crew. She'd been hoping since the beginning that he hadn't authored that

email, if only because it meant misfortune had be-
fallen his family. "No," she snapped. "What are you
doing now? Do you think you're a human lie detec-
tor?"

"Something like that."

If an altered voice could express a smug smile, his
did. Her mind filled with an image of the sexy, tuxe-
doed Parker Lawton at her door, lips curved in an in-
viting smile rather than set into an irritated slash. Her
hormones took a sudden side trip down kissing lane.

What was wrong with her? They weren't holding hands, he wasn't trying to romance her, he was
monitoring her responses for truthfulness.

"Do you or the network ever trace anonymous
informants?"

She stifled the first instinct to cooperate. He was
treading into territory that would make lawyers
salivate. "I've cooperated enough. It's your turn to
share."

"You don't want to hear my secrets."

"Yes, I do," she insisted, seizing a chance to go
on the offensive. "Did you steal gold while you were
in Iraq, Lawton?"

"What will you do if you find out I'm not who
you think I am?"

Another evasion. "Turn on the lights and prove it."

"I'll give you a truth." His fingertips slid up a few

inches and back down again to settle once more. Had he felt her pulse skip in response? "I have no intention of keeping you here any longer than necessary."

Why did his emphasis on *necessary* create a swirl of warm temptation low in her belly? She scolded herself for not being revolted by his audacity. She should be resisting. Fighting. Taking action to get out of here. "Shall we define necessary?"

"Not unless you're a lawyer," he deadpanned. "I'm well aware of your position with the network, your college degrees and your grades all the way back to kindergarten. Seems you were a real chatterbox as a kid."

Now, *that* upset her. He had no right to go tearing through her life. Her work, yes. Her past and her childhood? No way. "You—"

"Cowardly bastard? I've been called worse," he said. "You might be right. Tell me how the network would track down a source that doesn't want to be found."

"No." She shifted as far from him as he allowed. It wasn't nearly enough. "Let me go or leave. I'm done talking."

"I need information, Rebecca."

Her shoulders slumped, defeated. "If you don't like what I have to say, let me go. Surely you have the skills and gadgets to keep an eye on me in the real world."

"Watching you isn't my point. I need to know you're safe while I'm gathering information. The sooner you tell me everything you know about the source, the sooner I'll let you go."

"Everything?"

"Yes. What I don't know could hurt both of us."

She fidgeted under his fingertips, seeking a bit more space. A little distance would restore her sanity. He kept his fingers on the sensitive skin, his body close enough to catch her every twitch and flinch.

"In reverse order," she began, "everything I know about this situation amounts to filing charges with the police the minute you let me out of this room."

"I'm not surprised. Go on."

Not surprised and not concerned. "I also know you're a jerk."

"So noted. Get to the part that led us to this point."

"You led me here," she muttered. "Where are we anyway?"

"Rebecca."

She sighed. Fighting him was getting her nowhere, better to just tell him and let the chips fall. At some point, her captor would make a mistake. She had to believe that much.

"Anonymous tips are the worst. I told you that

before." Now she was repeating herself. "Bill and I started fact-checking the tip itself. We learned the unit accused of the gold theft was in the area at the time of the alleged theft. Parker Lawton was part of that unit, just as the tipster claimed." Did his breath catch? Oh, she hoped she was making him nervous.

"The family name caught my attention. Bill and I got to know them as well as differing cultures and a few brief days allowed. They didn't project the wealth I would expect to go with the amount of gold stolen. They were kind, helpful and articulate."

She had to stop for a steadying breath, deciding how she wanted to explain it to him. "So this tip comes in and we start working it."

"Because you were angry for the family?" he asked.

"Because exposing appalling behavior is the right thing to do," she countered.

"You're eager to assume the worst of those soldiers," he said.

"Not true. The show is about giving viewers a compelling, objective story." She paused, trying to dial down the defensive tone. "We've been doing our research. Did you know *one* man on that team has a fortune? He's inexplicably wealthy," she added, wishing she could see his face. "As in one day he was an average guy, and almost overnight he was a billionaire. That in itself is suspicious."

He snorted. "Suspicious isn't proof. Go on."

Go on. Why did that two-word directive slip over her skin like silk, even with the creepy voice alteration device? "You saw the email from the source. There were six names on the list. Bill and I divided the research to speed things along. So far Lawton hasn't agreed to speak with Bill on the record. He will, though, won't he?"

"No idea."

"The night of the gala, the night you kidnapped me, Bill called me from a diner where he was waiting to meet the former CO of the team. The guy was late. What did you do, warn him off?"

"You're mistaken."

She laughed, the sound disappearing into the dark. "Please. I know it's you, Lawton." *Please don't let it be anyone else.* "Who else has any cause to hold me hostage?" She thought of the man with the scar and the brutal grip. "I can't imagine another thief taking this much interest in me or the show. I'm not an idiot, Lawton." She had to get him to slip up and admit it.

"I'm not Lawton."

"Maybe not," she said, pretending to consider. It was difficult to sell the nonchalant bravado effectively with only her voice while he hovered close enough to catch every reaction. "I had it on good authority *he* is a stand-up guy. You sure aren't."

"Tell me more about the family you think lost the gold. The source gave you a pretty common name."

That caught her off guard. Had he known them well too? "Why don't we work together? The show is objective, remember? Together we can probably figure out who the source is. We can even tell your side, and if the men on the list are really innocent, we'll make that clear."

He made another disbelieving sound, accompanied by one more adjustment of his fingers on her pulse points. "You'd work with me? A man you believe is connected to an army unit who stole from your friends?"

"Yes." She needed to sell the lie, had to convince him she could be an asset. Once she got out of this room, she'd turn him over to the first cop she saw. "You've done your homework. You know we work with all sorts of people to get to the heart of a story. I'd work with the devil himself if it gets me out of here."

"The devil, me, but not your dad. Interesting."

Taking a play out of his book, she left that assertion unanswered.

"I'm not the devil," he said, his voice tight. "You

should know Bill didn't get his interview. Theo Manning is dead."

What? She swiveled her head around to look at him, the effort futile in the darkness. "No," she murmured. "How? When?" He was only trying to shock her. Still, she felt her heart clutch, worried he might be telling her the truth. He couldn't mean it.

"Murdered on Thursday night, thanks to *your* research," he continued. "Jeff Bruce, second on that list, is in the hospital. It wasn't an accident. You, Rebecca, are a threat to all the men on that list. You'll stay *right here*."

His fingers lifted from her wrists and he caught both her hands in one of his. She felt a flare of fear and in the next moment the bindings were gone, her hands free. Her back, the air around her, cooled as he retreated. She hadn't even heard him open a knife or tool capable of slicing though the zip ties so smoothly. Maybe it was a secret trick he'd learned in the army.

His stealth was almost worse than the absolute control he held. He'd clearly thought through each step. Maybe he'd done something like this before, yet nothing in Parker Lawton's background indicated he was a serial kidnapper or worse. Nothing they'd found so far, anyway.

Other than his instant leap from middle class to

wealthy, nothing indicated he was anything other than an honorable veteran. The opposing pictures painted by the anonymous source and the first layer of facts had made her want to dig deeper into Lawton, with or without an end story in mind. Now not so much.

Once more logic fed the doubt that had taken root in her mind. What if the man in control of this room and her life wasn't Lawton, but some crazy thug he'd hired to interrogate her?

"Thanks," she said, rubbing her wrists where his hands had been. The zip ties chafed her pride more than her skin, and releasing her was a move that showed trust. *Or pure arrogance*, a little voice in her head pointed out. "If you prove the tip is bogus, I won't even press charges." She lied openly now that he wasn't close enough to catch the deception. "At the very least, let's have the rest of this conversation with the lights on."

She heard the soft whir of the lock as the door opened and closed again. The lights came up and she turned a circle, blinking as her eyes adjusted to the light, searching for him. "Oh, come on!" She did another full circle, as if by willing it she could make him reappear.

"We'll talk again," the voice carried through the speakers.

She leaped for the door and hammered it with her fists. "You jerk! You need me out there!"

"We're all safer with you in there. I'll be back in a few hours."

Hours! With no windows or clocks, she had no idea what time that would be in the real world. "Wait!" She wouldn't let him go without getting *something* in return.

"What is it?" he queried.

"When you come back, be polite." Considering the vast imbalance of power here, she probably should have phrased that as a question rather than a demand.

"How so?"

Oh, good, he was still out there, listening. "Give the lights a flicker or say hello before tumbling me into the dark. Please," she added belatedly. She pointed at the upended water glass she'd hit when he turned out lights. "The floor you save might be your own."

In the corner, the tiny red light on the camera flashed. "Okay." The speaker clicked and the camera light winked out.

He was gone. She knew it even without making a request or comment that would go unanswered. The red light was out on the camera too. She assumed that meant he wasn't watching all the time, only when the light was on. She could find a way to use that.

She'd thought she had him on the hook while they were talking, and he'd wriggled off again. He was out there chasing something and she was stuck. Was Theo Manning really dead? She rubbed the heel of her hand over the ache in her chest. Whatever was going on out there, Lawton couldn't keep her here indefinitely. He had to know that as well as she did.

While she still believed it was most likely the man holding her was Lawton, she didn't *know*. Didn't have any proof.

She had to admit to herself that the search to corroborate the anonymous email combined with a friend's death—if that was true—might have pushed a man like Lawton over the edge. She could have a better idea of who she was dealing with if her dad had helped her get a look at the service records.

That didn't answer why he'd locked her up in here. If Lawton wasn't the man holding her, she might be in dire trouble. This guy could be as much of a nutcase as her captivity suggested. Dwelling on that scenario only fed the smoldering panic inside her that was all too ready to leap into a consuming inferno of debilitating fear.

Becca combed her hands through her hair and took slow, deep breaths until the sensation passed. Then she stalked up and down the room with a renewed determination to save herself and break out of here.

Chapter Six

"Another dead end," Parker told the empty room. On a weary oath, he pushed back from the wobbly table and stood up from the lousy excuse for a chair. Crossing the small room in two strides, he carefully peered through the crack in the window curtains. No one visible on the nearby rooftops, and down on the street the cars seemed to be a fresh crop than those he'd passed when he walked into the shabby motel a few hours ago.

He longed for the assistance and conveniences of his office, his condo or even the rental outside the safe room, but he needed to be as unpredictable as the enemy. Staying in one place too long or going back too frequently only made it easier for whoever was picking off his team.

Exhausted, frustrated, he wanted to get out in

the city to walk and think. And yes, to tempt anyone who might be on his tail. The remainder of the night invited him to search for his opponent's weak point and go on the attack. Except he didn't know where to start looking. San Francisco, Nevada or somewhere in between?

After he'd studied the rest of her raw notes, it was clear Rebecca had told him everything about Iraq and it still wasn't enough to connect any of the dots. Although it would be easy to believe she'd held some essential detail back for the sake of insurance, he knew better.

It had taken him hours to recover from that conversation. Not only because she called him by name and she'd been so open and candid about her experiences overseas. No. It had been the citrus scent of her hair, the fragile skin covering her pounding pulse points. Her defiance and courage despite the odds blew him away and drew him closer simultaneously.

Her pulse had remained steady under his fingertips. Fast with nerves, but steady. Her voice, that cool, cultured sound rippling over him through the darkness, had held the unyielding tone of a woman who knew she was right. Until she'd heard Theo died. Her pulse had gone haywire, stuttering under his fingertips as she processed the news.

He should let her go. Beg her forgiveness. And he

would. As soon as he could figure out if he would be doing it for her or to invite the scarred man back for another attempt to nab her. Until he could trust himself with that decision, until he could own it, she'd stay safely tucked away. "Locked away," he amended aloud.

What a fool! How had he let a rescue turn into this nightmare? He could just hear the men he'd worked so closely with on that last mission cackling over his idiocy. Theo's life motto had been Think First. He'd drilled it into everyone he served with as if it was his personal mission to teach others that no matter how bad things got, there was always time to think before taking an irreversible action.

Parker hadn't taken any time to think. He'd been reactionary from the moment he heard about Theo's murder. Before that, if he was honest. The blackmail note had set his mind spinning out of control. He hooked his thumbs into his back pockets and dropped his head in shame. Reactionary was a pretty word for glossing over an outright kidnapping.

The pure shock of seeing all their names in one place had unnerved him. Still did. The six of them had been deployed to the same base, working with their individual units, until Theo had gathered them for one particular covert operation.

They'd gone out in teams of three, and after more

than a month battling rough conditions and unforgiving terrain, they found and dispatched a terrorist cell moving explosives from Iran to Iraq. No one should ever have put all six names together. It should have been impossible. Except someone had proved it was possible, compounding that problem by creating a compelling story designed to discredit all of them unless Parker paid the blackmail.

He glanced back to the table where her devices and his laptop sat open. None of his extensive searches were getting him closer to identifying the source behind this mess. The only thing he labeled progress was discovering that the driver who'd run Jeff off the road couldn't be Fadi, the young man from the village near the Iranian border. No matter what Jeff thought he saw, Parker's expert at the office had used amateur radio operators to confirm that the kid was still in Iraq with his family. Too bad he hadn't found a way to ask if the family still had their gold.

Parker rubbed at his temples, astonished at how small the world had become. It was nearly incomprehensible that he and Rebecca had met the same lanky eighteen-year-old within a few weeks of each other. Fadi had served as a translator first for Parker's team and then Rebecca's crew. Logic said someone from that village was behind this, and yet the setup was too sophisticated, the knowledge too complete and the reach too long.

That left him wondering if someone on the base had learned about their operation. If so, what was the end game here? It couldn't be about the money or Theo would still be alive and Jeff would be home with his wife. And how did kidnapping Rebecca fit in?

He prowled around the shabby motel room and checked in on Rebecca. He'd expected her to be sleeping and found she was marking time in a similar pattern of pent-up frustration in the safe room. He turned up the audio and heard her cursing him in increasingly innovative combinations. As he watched, he wondered if it would take all of his fortune to buy her forgiveness. Rush, reportedly the wealthiest man in the city, might not have enough money to buy that woman's forgiveness.

No, money wasn't the right key to her anyway. She'd offered to pay off her captor, and a quick search of her financials proved she had a hefty nest egg at her disposal. Rebecca's world revolved around the story. Would admitting he was better at being a security expert and a soldier than a wealthy civilian win her forgiveness?

The story. Parker kept circling back to that. The blackmailer claimed the media had been informed of the story. Yet no one had run it. None of his remaining friends on the list had received calls from other reporters. Only Rebecca's group had started investigating, and they'd interpreted the sudden leap in his net worth as a smoking gun.

The tip in itself could have been a story worthy of a network mention. If her reporter had run with the first suggestion of the story, tossing out inflammatory accusations of corruption, as many might have done in their places, the men on that list would be facing tough questions right now. All of them embarrassed, scrutinized and investigated, blindsided by a media feeding frenzy. Who would gain from that? And why now?

With Theo dead and Jeff still in the hospital, restitution for the stolen gold didn't seem to be the primary objective at all.

His phone chirped and hummed on the table and Parker hesitated, not sure he could handle more bad news. In his experience no one called with good news at nearly one o'clock in the morning. The screen showed the call was from Tony, one of the men he'd assigned to keep an eye on Rebecca's apartment in Russian Hill.

"What is it?" Parker asked.

"Flashlight moving around," Tony replied, his voice low. "Someone is searching the place."

"You didn't see anyone go in?"

"Whoever is in there didn't use the door."

Parker stifled the first knee-jerk response. He wanted to send Tony in and have him haul the burglar to the office so Parker could conduct an interrogation.

Think first. "Call the police," he said to Tony. "Do what you can to get a picture and tail whoever leaves the apartment."

"On it," Tony said, ending the call.

Parker pocketed his phone and worked through the next steps. Russian Hill wasn't in Detective Baird's district, but Parker could make sure he caught wind of the break-in once they had more information. Tony knew how to call in a crime without sharing contact information and he was as good as a ghost at following people. With the apartment empty, they didn't need to worry about endangering anyone.

Glaring at Rebecca's tablet, Parker returned to the table and closed it. The missing pieces of this puzzle weren't there. Nor were they in the human-interest story she and Bill had brought back from Iraq. He couldn't write off the places where her journey and his had almost collided as coincidence.

Someone was pulling on strings Parker couldn't see, jerking them around like puppets. Her show. His mission. Where did they overlap? He was sure

her show was being used as a pawn in the effor~~~ ~~
disgrace him and his team, but she'd also been targeted personally.

There was a way to get in front of this. With only
two days left, he needed a comprehensive plan to protect her as well as the three other men on the list. He
couldn't dump them all into safe rooms.

He sank into the chair and leaned forward into
the table, propping his head on his fists. He'd been
through everything, too many times to count. If she
talked with army units during her trip to Iraq, those
notes weren't on this device. It was a question to ask
when he went back to the safe room.

He used the app to check on her again. She was
sprawled across the Murphy bed. He watched for a
minute, trying to decide if she was really asleep or
faking it for the cameras. Observing her while she
was vulnerable made him feel like the worst creep.
He switched the view, found the camera fritzed out
and took it as a sign to stop being an idiot with her.
He used the app to check the cameras outside the
building, relieved when he didn't see anything remarkable.

He should sleep as well. Instead, he started a new
search on his laptop, looking at the world headlines
during the days and weeks when Rebecca's crew and

his unit were in the same vicinity. Then he saw it: 12 Dead—Village Caught in Cross Fire.

The date of the article matched up, and his blood turned cold, slogging through his veins. Not the village where Rebecca and Bill had been, farther north on the border. The article claimed Iranian smugglers had been outed to US forces and had retaliated against the community to make a point.

Oh, he should have suspected this involved the off-the-books skirmish at the border. He would have thought of this tragedy first, if there had been any survivors. He swore. At the time Jeff, Matt and he had been certain they'd cut off the head of that snake. Someone had clearly survived.

Parker stared up at the water-stained ceiling and replayed the entire week in his mind. It wasn't the first time and it definitely wouldn't be the last time those harrowing moments consumed him. Knowing he couldn't sleep, he reached for his phone and dialed Franklin Toomey, the third name on the list. He stared at the contact listing for a long time but never hit the Call icon.

He'd warned Frank and the others yesterday. The man was on guard. These new details could wait until a reasonable hour.

The blackmail note sent to him made sense now. Raw fear iced Parker's skin. The restitution demand had little to do with money or family and everything to do with honor. It was about vengeance, and more innocent lives would get caught in the cross fire. Who had the intel, the reach and the nerve to start picking off soldiers on American soil?

Of the six of them, only Theo would have had the names of likely suspects. Killing him immediately made sense now. Kidnapping Rebecca might have been a ham-fisted attempt to force her network to run the story. Instead, the scarred man had pulled Parker right into the heart of his deadly game.

Up against one or more highly-skilled assassins on American soil, Parker needed to dig deep. Gathering intel was step one. Security was step two. Too bad for his Iranian enemy, Parker happened to be an expert in both areas.

He focused his efforts on drawing out and identifying the scarred man, mining every source and latent surveillance camera for more information on Theo's death and Jeff's accident. Skilled or not, everyone left a trail of some sort. Parker drafted an email asking a favor of another friend who'd transitioned from the army and landed with Homeland Security. Maybe they had some intelligence on the man with the scar. He paused, thinking through all the pros and cons before he hit Send.

After catching a much-needed nap and making

more phone calls, Parker was convinced he'd found the first bread crumbs on that trail. His friend at Homeland agreed to help, and the hotel where the awards gala had been held invited him down to look through the surveillance footage from that night.

Though the Iranians had a head start, he would catch up. He sent a few replies in Rebecca's name to the emails that seemed most urgent and then closed down her computer. Checking the window once more, he had to give the Iranians points for subtlety. If they were tracking the activity on her accounts or the devices, they were being exceptionally discreet.

He packed the gear he'd brought to the motel room, leaving only a few bread crumbs behind. If the roles were reversed, he would search the vacated room of his enemy. With luck, they'd believe he was off his game and follow his bogus clue, giving him a couple of hours to launch an offensive plan.

Luck failed him. A tail caught up with his SUV within blocks of the hotel. At least it looked that way. He checked his mirrors and swore with mild frustration.

Driving through the city congestion on the weekend had pros and cons. It was easier to lose a tail, but more difficult to confirm one. He just couldn't be sure the midsize white sedan one car back from him now was following him with a purpose. It was possible he was simply overtired and paranoid. Despite the low odds of figuring this out on his own, he had to try. He couldn't lead the killers behind the blackmail note and false story to where he was keeping Rebecca safe.

What he wouldn't give to be back overseas where support and reliable intel were a secure radio call away. He turned onto a famous street no local in his right mind would travel willingly and gently slalomed right and left to navigate the one-way intersections. The white car followed.

At the last possible moment, he swerved into the turn lane for the next block, and the white car followed again. To his right another driver blew through the now-red traffic light to a chorus of angry car horns and squealing brakes.

He glanced up at the traffic camera installed on the light pole to help the city catch drivers misbehaving. Belatedly, he remembered he wasn't nearly as alone as he felt.

Upon his latest inspection this morning, his SUV hadn't been tagged with GPS or any other surveillance devices. Pressing the button on his steering wheel, he called Sam at the Gray Box office. Sam could hack into any system, including the city's traffic cameras. Back when Sam and Rush were setting up protective measures against corporate espionage attempts to steal their tech and worse, Sam had created a specific route through the city so they could both pinpoint pesky surveillance tails and lose them as needed.

"Bellemere," Sam answered on the third ring.

"It's Parker," he said. "I may or may not have a shadow out here in the city today. Can you help me out?"

"Of course. What's your location?"

Parker heard the eagerness in Sam's voice and replied quickly, even as he kept one eye on the white sedan in his wake. "I'm in my SUV," he added.

"All right," Sam said. "Give me a minute." It only took a few seconds. "Okay, I can see you. Hmm. Take your next right."

"Got it." Parker could practically hear Sam cracking his knuckles. "I think it's the white sedan two car lengths back."

Sam hummed thoughtfully again. "Why don't you cruise out toward the Presidio? Do you remember the route we set up on that side of town?"

"Well enough," Parker said, picturing the convoluted path in his head.

"Great. Drive happy, my friend. I've got your back. In a minute I should have his registration."

Parker kept the line open, though neither he nor Sam spoke while Parker drove the route. The white sedan, or one like it, stayed close the entire time. No way this was a coincidence. In the quiet car, he second-guessed himself. Any smart team would be subtle about tailing him. They'd trade off every few blocks, or hang back. Whoever drove the sedan didn't seem to care whether or not Parker knew he was back there.

"According to the plate, the car has a California registration and is insured with a rider for one of those rideshare things."

"Do you think the person on my tail is a fare?" If so, he could try and request any records from the driver.

"Not exactly. There's no one other than the driver in the car. The view from the last traffic cam is pixelated, but I doubt the car's owner, one Jenny Swanson, has a thick dark beard."

Neither did the scarred man or the man running interference for the attempted kidnapping at the gala. Did they steal Jenny's car or was she a connection to the team giving his team fits? "So I'm being followed."

"That may or may not be the good news," Sam agreed. "You want me to keep running this down?"

"Please," Parker answered. His mind was moving on to the next part of his problem. He wanted to get

Rebecca out of the city before the assassin tracked her down again.

"And?"

Parker hesitated, unsure what he was supposed to say. "Thank you?"

"Very mannerly, although not what I was fishing for." Sam chuckled. "It was a prompt for you to ask for more help. I can send an alert to the police. You'd have some breathing space."

"No, thanks. I'd rather know exactly where this guy is."

"You got it."

When the call ended, he aimed for the condo again, careful to keep the white sedan in sight as he worked through his dwindling options.

If he didn't get Rebecca to a new hiding place soon, he had no doubt she'd get caught in the cross fire. Rescuing her had been tricky enough. Talking with her had created an entirely different and unexpected set of problems, none of which he could resolve while she viewed him as the enemy.

What he'd learned during his background search on her left him reluctant to just walk in, introduce himself and beg for her understanding. Although she had a mile-wide streak of compassion, she also held grudges. In his case, she should. He deserved each and every terrible thought and word she aimed at him.

He liked her too much. The courage and creativity she showed trying to outwit him and escape made him want to stand back and let her win. Should he do that? he wondered. Should he let her escape without any confirmation of her captor's identity? A safe option, but for some twisted reason, he didn't want to confirm he was the coward she'd labeled him.

While he debated his best approach, formulating a story Rebecca might embrace, he circled the block twice. Someone had been brave enough to take his designated parking space on the side street.

Making sure the driver on his tail was following closely, Parker aimed for the dry cleaner to pick up the dress he'd dropped off yesterday. With any luck the gesture would give Rebecca pause before she filed a report with the police. He didn't bother with a meal, since he was about to insist she hide elsewhere. He didn't expect her to let him off the hook for kidnapping. His behavior had been atrocious, his knee-jerk decisions lousy.

No, she had every right to file charges against him. The catch would be convincing her to grant him a few days to get this team of assassins out of the US before they killed anyone else. Although the police department was capable, they were no match for the coming battle, and Parker sure couldn't stop anyone if he was buried under a mountain of paperwork and complaints in a county lockup.

Chapter Seven

When the lights flickered, twice, and then went out as her captor heeded her request, Becca readied herself to fight. Today was the day she'd break free of this room. He'd been in this room with her. She had a sense of his size and power. She would have one chance, one moment when surprise was on her side. She had to make this work or he might never let her go no matter what he'd said that first night. Reminding herself she'd be fighting Lawton, she bounced a little on her bare feet. Whether or not it was true, she had to believe she was going up against someone who'd once had morals and might pull a punch rather than hurt an innocent woman.

Overnight, she'd done what she could to interfere with the camera feeds, without making it obvious she was the root of the trouble. When the red lights were out, she'd balanced on her suitcase, scraping and prying at the lenses, half-afraid he'd burst through the door and tie her up. That approach hadn't worked, so she'd resorted to using the tweezers from her toiletry case to work on the screws in the brackets. Once the brackets were loose, she jammed her metal nail file into the nest of wires behind the camera by the door and hoped for the best.

"Step back from the door," the menacing, altered voice rumbled through the speaker.

She obeyed, silently lamenting whatever sensor or gadget kept him informed of her actions in here. Did he have it wired for infrared too?

The door opened with the familiar near-silent whoosh and she heard the rustle of plastic. Her heart stuttered in her chest. Though he'd never really laid a hand on her, she feared that was about to change. Permanently. She'd seen enough true-crime documentaries and read enough fiction thrillers to know the preferred material for containing evidence of a murder was plastic.

She tried to rein in her racing imagination. While it was hard to accept that a veteran with Lawton's record would kill her in cold blood, it wasn't an unprecedented situation. People went off the rails every day, and she suspected very few of them had his motivation of keeping millions of dollars in gold.

Her skin went hot and then cold and she trembled, faced with the daunting task of survival. She would not become a victim without a fight that left her mark on *him*. She refused to die alone and unheard in this horrible room with all its comfortable amenities.

Holding her breath, she heard only his footfalls, the plastic and the whisper of the door moving on those unbeatable, industrial hinges. Timing her attack based on the way he'd entered on previous visits, she waited until he was through the door to strike.

She didn't do the obvious lunge for the open door. He had to be prepared for that option. No, she kicked the small ottoman behind him into the gap, praying it would be enough to prevent the door from closing.

Only a faint sliver of light from whatever was beyond the door illuminated the space. It was more than she'd seen during his past visits, and she used the variations in the shadows to sort out her captor's shape within the dark room. Riding a tide of desperate determination, she threw herself at him, aiming her shoulder at his midsection. He angled away, but she got enough of him to shove him back against the love seat.

As much as she wanted to pummel him or turn on the lights and demand answers, she scrambled for the door. Escape was her top priority. Five steps was all she needed to reach the door from the love seat. Five steps and she'd be on the other side looking for a cop. Let the police sort out who her captor was, how he'd brought her here and why. The state prosecutors could have a field day with him in court.

"Stop!"

No way. The heavy vaultlike door was fighting the ottoman, and winning, based on the scrape and snap of the wooden legs. She had mere seconds to make her escape. Two more strides and her ordeal was over.

He caught her ankle and dragged her back. She screamed in despair, kicking him hard enough in the shoulder to make him grunt with pain. Up again, she'd taken only one stride before he had one arm locked around her midriff. He turned her to face him and part of his arm slid over her breast. On reflex, she slapped him.

The loud crack of her hand against his face startled them both. The pure-luck shot gave her another opening. She used it, but he caught her again. She screamed for help, using her best horror flick scream. Someone must be within earshot outside this room. Though she fought him with everything, hands, hair clip, fingernails, knees, elbows and feet, he kept gaining the advantage. Her arms flailed as she reached for any object to fend him off. Nothing worked.

Even with the adrenaline shooting through her system, she was outmatched. He had every advantage from size and reach to home court. She found herself caught between the wall and his body.

"Settle down!" he snapped. "I won't hurt you."

"Yet." She tried again to knee him in the groin and missed. Again.

He swore as she launched into one more round of shrieking hostility. His expertise versus her will to survive. It shouldn't have been a shock that expertise won. He won.

She found herself pinned to the cold tile floor by his hot, hard body. His hands manacled her wrists and his legs pressed the full length of hers. In the almost near dark, her mind started cataloging the details of his build. Clearly her captor kept himself in excellent shape and she wondered if the calluses she felt on his hands were from the gym or some kind of honorable work.

And why did it matter? Her escape attempt had failed miserably, and whether or not this was Parker Lawton she knew she wouldn't have another chance. Thinking of the plastic, she felt the first tears leak from her eyes. It was over. She coughed out a sob of despair, despite her best efforts to go out strong.

"Lights to dim." The voice alteration was gone and the clear, deep voice giving the order swirled around her like a sensual fog. That he didn't sound the least bit winded while her breath sawed in and out of her lungs made her want to start fighting all over again.

The small pinpoints of light in the ceiling came up in clusters and illuminated the room, confirming her suspicions. Parker Lawton was her captor. He stared down at her, apparently in no hurry to move from his position on top of her. Relief and temper warred for dominance while her traitorous body enjoyed every sensation. Her gaze drifted from his dark eyes to his full lips, and for a long moment she wondered how those lips would feel on hers.

"Rebecca?" Her name in his normal voice sounded strange, broke the spell she'd fallen under.

"Get off me!" She swallowed a fresh burst of frustrated tears and bucked and twisted under him, to no avail. "You did this!" Furious, she flung a string of obscenities at him until her breath was gone. With him on top of her, she couldn't quite get her lungs refilled. "Why?" she gasped.

"Take it easy." He levered himself up just enough for her to breathe. "I'm not here to hurt you."

He already had, in more ways than she cared to admit. She had always believed she was strong and smart. Then he'd come along and kidnapped her from a public building and held her against her will. She hated the things she'd considered doing to gain her freedom.

"I'm going to press charges," she said with as much dignity as she could muster. She glared up at him as he hopped to his feet. She was already feeling the effects of their fight. "By this time next year, I'll own your security company and anything else with your name on it."

"Probably." He held out a hand to help her up and she batted it away.

His easy acceptance of her claim was the equivalent of pouring gasoline on a fire. "How long have you kept me here?" she demanded, standing up without any help from him.

"Too long. You're free to go."

Her knees nearly buckled with relief. She leaned into the love seat for support. "Do you mean it?"

He nodded, tucking his hands into his pockets. "I want to explain a few things before you go."

The red imprint of her hand on his cheek gave her a little satisfaction. She was still outraged that anyone thought they could smother a story by holding her here in a safe room. That he was a veteran honorably discharged with combat hero medals made it worse.

"Start talking while I pack." The statement was ludicrous, but she owned it, turning around to gather up the belongings she hadn't expected to take with her.

"I have your phone, uh, in my car."

"How convenient for *you*." She didn't want to know what he thought he'd found in her call history and the other apps. He'd picked through her life, she knew that from his questions. She slid a look over her shoulder at his continued silence and caught him looking through the sketches she'd made. "Stop that. Hand it over."

He shook his head, flipping the pages back and forth, engrossed in her drawings.

"It's private," she said, resisting the urge to stomp her foot like a three-year-old. "Like a journal." She made a grab for it and he swiveled out of her reach.

"You're good," he said absently.

"Gee, thanks." *Ignore it, ignore him,* she coached herself, zipping her suitcase. "Open the door."

He held up the notepad and used his phone to take pictures of the pages. "Stop that," she said.

To her surprise he did stop. He held out the notepad, open to the page she'd devoted entirely to sketches of the man with the scar. "Do you know this man?" His eyes held the same worry she recalled from the night of the awards gala.

She took a half step back, unnerved by his intensity and the mean eyes leering at her from the page. "No. Do you?"

"But you've seen this man," he pressed.

"Obviously we both have," she replied.

"Where did you see him?"

"At the awards gala. He reeked of onions." She gripped the handle of her suitcase. "Open the door, Lawton."

"Call me Parker."

She wouldn't. "Open the door."

"Have you seen him anywhere else in town? Do you remember what he did to you?"

Becca squared her shoulders and set her teeth against the tremor that threatened at his questions. She remembered feeling caught and the scent of onions overpowered by something sweeter, stronger. "No," she lied. She didn't owe Lawton anything. "Open. The. Door."

He handed her the notepad. "I am sorry, Rebecca, for everything." Stepping to the panel, he pressed his hand to the screen. There was a soft beep, and then he did something else and the door swung open.

She hurried by him, stopping short when she found herself in someone's magnificent home. "Have you been right out here the whole time?" She gazed around the gorgeous, modern decor of the condo, drank in the wide view of the ocean. Freedom had never looked so wonderful.

His eyebrows flexed and, smart man, he didn't take his gaze off her. "Here in the condo? No."

She pushed away the flood of questions about

his whereabouts, focusing on the most important issue. "I'm leaving. You can keep the phone. I plan to burn everything you've touched once I'm home." She started for the door.

"I'll let you leave once we come to terms."

She plowed forward, determined to get as far from him as possible, until she saw the security panel at the front door as well. Naturally, when she tried the doorknob, it was useless.

"Terms?" She folded her arms over her chest. "I will only agree that I won't kill you for this. Everything else is fair game." She held up a hand when he shifted his feet. "Hold still," she ordered. "I mean it. I can get this story out and moving with a single email. I can ruin you, your company—"

"You can," he said as if it wouldn't bother him in the least. "Or you could listen."

Listen? She'd been listening since he locked her in here. He'd terrified her, shocked her and annoyed her. She was done playing this game his way.

He moved again and she braced to fend off an attack. Her gaze locked on the dry cleaning bag on the floor behind him, just inside the safe room. *That* was the plastic she'd heard in the darkness. He turned slightly, following her gaze. He plucked it from the floor and smoothed the plastic and the fabric, then draped it neatly over the back of one of the dining room chairs.

"That's my dress."

"Yes."

"You had my dress dry-cleaned?" Her gaze darted from the bag to him and back again. "When?" Why couldn't she figure out if he was a good guy or a bad guy? What kind of kidnapper would be so thoughtful?

The sick kind, she told herself. He'd held her against her will for two days? Three? She had no real way of knowing aside from the meals. Her thoughts were pinballing through her mind. "How long has it been?"

"Almost two days," he said, his gaze steady. "It's Saturday morning."

She wanted to hate him for his steely composure as her self-control frayed. "It's already Saturday?" She thought of Bill's failed interview with Manning and her Thursday date. "Has anyone reported me missing?"

"No." He shifted. It was barely perceptible, but she was an expert at the subtleties of body language.

"Because you did what exactly?" She gestured for him to fill in the sentence.

"I've been managing your emails. The office thinks you're out of town dealing with a family emergency."

Only the calming methods she'd learned in yoga class kept her from launching herself at him. Well, that and the physical scuffle that proved she was grossly outmatched. The element of surprise had been her only advantage, and she sensed she would never have it again. Not with this man.

Figuring out who he was before she made her move didn't change what he was. He was a soldier, an expert in covert operations and financially blessed by fair means or foul along the way. She took a step toward him. "Did you steal the gold?"

"No." His gaze was steady and the sorrow in his dark brown eyes was obvious. "No one on that list has ever stolen anything." He gestured for her to sit down.

She remained where she was.

"I know this isn't ideal," he began.

"Which part?" By sheer willpower, she kept her hands loose when she wanted to ball them into fists. "Being held against my will or being able to identify you as my captor?"

"None of it is ideal," he snapped. "Please sit down."

She shook her head. "Not here. Not until I'm far away from that obnoxiously tiny room. Just say what you need to say so I can leave." She was coming dangerously close to begging again.

A crack of laughter startled her and she aimed her notorious glare at him. At the network, it was the expression known to silence argumentative reporters and send interns scurrying for the nearest shelter. He only laughed again. "What's so funny?"

"This. Us." He tipped his head toward her. "I imagine that scowl works on most people."

"It does, yes."

He bobbed his chin as if seeing the merits. "If our lives weren't on the line, it might have worked on me."

"Don't patronize me."

His slashing dark eyebrows lifted a fraction. "You make patronizing sound worse than kidnapping." He sat down and leaned back into the cushions of the plush sofa. "Yes, the doors are locked right now. You will be allowed to leave once you understand the stakes."

"I can take care of myself."

"I believe you. In most circumstances, you wouldn't need me at all." He shook his head. "This is different."

She suppressed a shiver at the hard edge in his voice. She took a seat on the edge of the black sofa facing him. Her body thrummed with tension from head to toe. "Get to the point. I have a couple days' worth of work to catch up on before Monday."

"First, please accept my apology. Kidnapping you

was a knee-jerk reaction. It started as a rescue and just spiraled out of control. I regret how you've been inconvenienced by my fear-based decisions."

She couldn't imagine him afraid of much of anything. "Are you afraid of me?"

He nodded, a rueful smile on his lips. "On a few levels."

A rescue—her mind latched on to that detail, refusing to let go. She crossed her legs at the knee and let her foot swing a little as she studied him. He meant it and his sincerity knocked her further off balance. "Then why did you do it?"

"Because I thought you could help me save my men," he explained. "Your reporter called my office. It raised red flags on my end." He sighed. "I wanted the name of the source who accused us of stealing. At the gala, the man with the scar grabbed you. He drugged you and was headed for the stairwell when I intervened."

"You didn't steal anything."

"No." Restless, he leaned forward and propped his elbows on his knees. "Unless we count stealing you from the scarred man."

"It counts." She just wasn't sure where to put the tally.

"Tell me what you remember about him," he said.

She bristled. "I'm not under your control or command anymore. In case you didn't notice, I've always been bad at taking orders."

His brown eyes flashed with something. Lust or temper? Either way, she was chagrined that the look sent a ripple of anticipation through her body. "I'm listening," she continued through the awkward silence. "You still haven't explained why you kept me here so long."

He reached behind him, and her breath caught, afraid he was pulling a weapon on her. Instead he held out an envelope that had been folded until the paper was nearly worn through at the creases.

"What's that?"

"Just read it." He inched closer, holding it out to her.

She took it but didn't open it right away. "Mr. Lawton—"

"The sooner you open the envelope the sooner you can get back to your life."

Parker Lawton had proven himself adept at several skills during her stay in his safe room. Deception topped the list, though his gift for igniting her temper was a close second. She stopped listing off his skills right there, before she could add his seductive voice and his ability to kindle her darkest sensual fantasies in absurd situations.

More annoyed with herself now than she was with

him, she opened the envelope and removed a half sheet of standard white copy paper. She read the brief message twice over, trying to make sense of it.

"Oh. We've been played," she began, her voice colliding with his. "Pardon me?"

His brow furrowed. "I said it's bogus," he replied. "Why are you on my side?"

"I'm not exactly on your side." *Yet.* The note, the *blackmail*, nudged her closer toward his corner. She dropped the note on the sofa and stood up, crossing the room to watch the ocean, needing some movement to think through the details. "You read the anonymous email I received, right?" she asked, without looking at him, still angry about the violation of her privacy.

"Yes," he admitted. "You believed it was from the family. Possibly from Fadi."

She nodded, her eyes on the waves moving with such constancy toward the shore. Watching the ocean soothed her. Always had. "The email was written to push my buttons, and the note was written to push yours." She turned to face him again. "It worked. Bill and I led the killer right to the targets they wanted."

"Once I read the email I was sure it was written by the same person who wrote the blackmail note," Parker said.

"I agree," she said, rubbing her hands over her

arms. "Fadi would never threaten to kill, especially not our soldiers. He was proud of how he helped the US."

"I thought the same," he said. "Come sit down a minute. We need to figure out why you were targeted."

She stayed put, keeping her back to the window and maintaining some much-needed distance. "Probably to mess with you," she suggested.

"I was thinking it was an attempt to force the story out."

She tipped her head to the side, considering. "Taking me removed your best access to the anonymous source. You'd come by the apartment earlier to hassle me. It might even have been an attempt to frame you."

"Hassle you? I only wanted to talk."

"And here we are." She spread her arms wide, let them fall to her sides. "Good job." He'd been cornered, his CO murdered and his best lead nearly captured. Sympathizing with him didn't excuse his actions, yet she understood why he'd done it. She fought that kernel of compassion. He didn't deserve it, not after scaring her and cuffing her and…her pulse was fluttering at the memory of his hands on her yesterday. She turned back to the ocean, willing herself to regain her common sense.

"I want to go home," she said. A hot shower, clean clothes and some tea would ease her sore muscles and pave the way for a good night's sleep in her own bed. In the safe room she'd been too nervous to really sleep.

"You shouldn't do that." Color flooded his face.

"Why not?"

"Someone was in your apartment last night. We don't know why yet."

With a groan, she held out her hand to make him stop. "Enough with the cloak-and-dagger routine. Just tell me, yes or no, is it safe for me to go home?"

"No." Worry flashed in his eyes again as he checked his phone. "The police are probably trying to reach you. We'll go see them first."

That explained his change of heart. "You're letting me go so the whole kidnapping thing won't come out."

"Not exactly." He stood up and retrieved the blackmail note, returning it to his wallet. Picking up her dress, he walked to the door, opening it wide. "You can tell the cops whatever you want, but we need to leave. Now."

"Why?"

He arched an eyebrow. "Didn't you just jump me to get out of here? You're free. Let's go."

His sudden urgency raised her suspicions. "I

didn't jump you," she protested hotly. "If I'm really free to go, I'm going home."

"You can't."

"Why not?" She wanted the pieces to fit together and give her a complete picture. She understood the investigative process, but she also understood the value of a narrative. "Tell me."

He pulled the door shut and programmed an electronic lock. "Because my best guess is the guy with the scar is an assassin working on behalf of someone powerful in Iran who blackmailed me and involved you."

For a moment, she just stood in the hallway, gawking at his back, then rushed forward to catch up before he reached the stairwell. "If you don't have the gold, why would the blackmailer think you could pay the ransom?" she asked in a low whisper.

"It's an excuse. He found out I have deep pockets, I guess." He shrugged and took her suitcase in his free hand as he marched down the stairs. "Think what a coup it would have been if I paid him off."

"How did your pockets get so deep?" She was close enough she could see that his jaw set and his breath caught. The question bothered him, though he hid it quickly. "I can research too."

"I know." He sighed. "I inherited a chunk of money just after I joined the army. Two friends gave me some excellent investment advice." The stairs let out into a small alcove and mail room for each of the three units. "Factor in that I was deployed with almost zero expenses, and it snowballed quickly, even while I set up my businesses."

No wonder he didn't flaunt his money; he'd never learned how. "Care to share your investment strategy?"

"No."

His deep voice rolled over her, pulling at her senses like an ocean wave. "Fine." Two could play the monosyllable game.

His eyes heated and his lips slanted into an expression caught between regret and frustration. Good grief, the expression left her wondering what she might have missed if they'd met under better circumstances. He said he'd rescued her and she believed him. He'd apologized as well, but still, actions had consequences.

Donning his ivy cap, he drew her aside. "My car's this way. I'll take you to the police station and then preferably to a friend's place to lie low. Have you decided if you'll wait or are you set on filing kidnapping charges against me today?"

"Why should I wait?" she asked, incredulous. "You removed me from my life for no valid reason."

"I had reason," he countered, his voice low and rough. "You were in danger."

"You could have taken me to a hospital," she said.

He didn't reply, his expression an inscrutable mask.

"You could have just talked to me."

He closed his eyes and murmured what might have been a quick prayer. "Just give me forty-eight hours. Please," he begged. "I can't stop the men hunting my team if I'm in jail."

The *please* landed on her heart with the weight of an anvil. "All right," she said. "I won't go to the police. Not about the kidnapping or the break-in."

His eyebrows dipped low over his eyes. "I didn't break in."

She gave her suitcase a spin. "You did at some point," she said with a syrupy smile.

The tops of his ears turned red. "Thank you, Rebecca."

"Call me Becca," she corrected. "And not so fast. You're not going hunting alone."

"You?" He started to laugh, but then the sound dried up. He leaned in, his voice intimidating without the device. "You'd drag those men through the mud for *ratings*?"

She swallowed back the instant lecture. He was stressed out and had just lost a good friend with another in the hospital. He deserved compassion and patience. If only there was someone else nearby who could offer him both. Someone he hadn't *kidnapped.* "The idea of an assassin with orders from Iran to attack soldiers on American soil is a major story. Yes, it would be nice to get the scoop, but more important than that," she pressed on when he tried to interrupt her, "is the safety of your team. You kidnapped me because you thought I could help. So why not let me help?"

"Because you're not qualified," he said. "We both know that." He started for the exit to the side street.

His flat dismissal jacked up her temper again. "We know nothing of the sort." She paused for a deep breath. "I was qualified enough to be kidnapped." She snapped her mouth shut and looked around for anyone listening. "You're innocent," she added. "Bill can tell your story better than anyone else."

"I don't need my story told." He shut his mouth and swiveled away. "I need to save the rest of my team. You can't help me with that."

There was more to this situation, details he was keeping locked up tight. For national security or personal reasons? Who was Parker Lawton under the impenetrable military past and the current security expertise? Why couldn't she shake this deep-seated need to find out?

She folded her arms, refusing to budge from her spot in the narrow hallway. "If you're shutting me out, I want your word you'll let me know what happens."

He rolled his eyes, swearing under his breath. "You'll know it turned out okay if you don't see my name or any of the others in the obituaries."

That wasn't the reassurance she was looking for. She was tired, sore and hungry. Rather than keep arguing, she figured the best way forward was for him to think he'd won this round. She probably shouldn't feel protective of the man who kidnapped her, even if it had started with a rescue.

However, she was perfectly content to feel protective of her nation, state and city. Parker might think he could do this alone, but someone needed to watch his back. She and Bill knew how to unravel rumors to find facts and locate people who didn't want to be found. By the time Parker realized she was still in the thick of it, it would be too late for him to shut her out.

Chapter Eight

The moment he turned up the lights in the safe room and revealed his face, Parker knew the charade was over. He understood her fury, gave her points for her cleverness as well as her elbow strike. The woman put up a good fight and he wanted to know what she'd done to his cameras. Beyond all that, he appreciated her resiliency and her willingness to write off his behavior as mindless stupidity rather than criminal intent. At least for the next two days.

Right now he just wanted to get out of the building before anyone saw them together. That would undermine every effort he'd made to create a plausible reason for her absence and break from the well-oiled routine. She could hardly be tending to a family crisis in a pricey condo with an ocean view.

Every time he looked at her, one of two things happened. Either he wanted to plunder her lush mouth or he wanted to apologize again for being an idiot. Since groveling only put him in a more precarious position and he was skating on thin enough ice at the moment, his brain kept returning to the kissing option.

Twice now he'd come close to giving in to that urge. Yesterday when he'd had her cuffed with zip ties and his hands on her silky skin had been a test of his willpower. Today was worse, after he'd finally subdued her attack. He wouldn't forget the feel of her sumptuous curves under his body any time soon. It was a wonder she hadn't snarled at him about his inappropriate desire or erection.

As she stood there stubbornly in the hallway, he thought she looked as delectable now in the snug jeans, college sweatshirt and worn high-top sneakers as she had in the dress he carried for her. She pursed her lips, rolling her daisy-tagged suitcase back and forth, and it was all he could do not to gather her into his arms, march back upstairs and lock them both in the safe room until they were too sated to move.

From a security standpoint, it wasn't a bad plan, actually. Even if the assassin found the condo, there would be no way through unless Parker willingly opened the door.

"What's that look about?" The natural wariness in her blue eyes brightened. "Did you change your mind?"

"No." He reached for the door. "You must be hungry. Come on."

He realized there were parts of his story she wasn't sure she could believe, and knowing who she was and what she did, he also knew she would do her best to figure them out. He had to convince her to drop it.

One crisis at a time, he thought, and at the moment the Iranians took precedence. Assuming he survived this insanity, he could find a way to distract her from digging too deeply into his real mission with Fadi and his family in Iraq. He was all for transparency, but not when it was sure to be misunderstood and freak out the general population. Sometimes good people had to do difficult things for the betterment of the world.

The door opened and the building maintenance man walked in. Parker forced a smile across his face and prayed for a distraction. "Good morning, Alan."

"Morning, Mr. Lawton. What a surprise."

"How's the wife?"

"Doing fine. You know, I—" Alan stopped and stared. At Becca. His genial expression transformed into a starstruck glow. "My goodness. Is it really you, Miss Wallace? The wife and I have watched every episode of your show," he gushed.

"Thank you, that's very kind." She extended her hand and let Alan give it a vigorous shake.

"My Sylvie will never believe it. Never." He patted his pockets and came up with his cell phone. "Would you mind terribly if I took a picture?"

"We really should be going," Parker said. Since when did television producers get celebrity status? "Maybe another time, Alan."

"Oh, don't listen to him. We have a few minutes." The gleam in Becca's eyes said it all. She wanted proof she'd been here as much as he didn't want to leave any evidence.

"How do you know each other?" Alan asked.

"I'll just take your suitcase out to the car," Parker said, resigned to his fate. He walked out while Alan asked her about a show last season, making Parker wonder how he kept each reporter and segment straight.

Returning to the building, he admired Becca's boundless patience even more when his snapped. Men he'd served with were in jeopardy. And with a soulless assassin on their trail, standing here in plain view, chatting up a storm, put all three of them in danger.

"Rebecca." He tipped his head toward the door.

She shifted in that direction, and Alan moved with her. Stifling a curse, Parker took her hand and guided her closer to the door. Alan didn't let up.

Though the white sedan was gone and he couldn't spot anyone on the street, Parker's instincts were snapping. Someone was watching them. Desperate to get out of here, to take whatever fight was coming away from Alan and the other innocent civilians in the neighborhood, he raised the key fob and pressed the button to start the SUV.

The big vehicle seemed to bounce on the tires and then the front end was immediately engulfed by a ball of flame. "Get down!" he shouted, knowing it was too late.

His vision registered the fiery explosion in slow motion long before the sound or the concussion wave from the blast blew out the glass door and window. The three of them were tossed around the hallway like leaves in a gale, and he did his best to shield Becca. The flash knocked the air from his lungs, and it felt as if someone had stuffed cotton in his ears. For long seconds all he could hear was the sound of his heart pounding.

Heat from the explosion pressed in on them, making it hard to breathe. Becca was under him again, her hands patting his face and arms. He asked if she was okay, but he couldn't hear her answer, only saw her nodding. She seemed generally unharmed, although her eyes were wide and swimming with tears, her face, hair and clothing covered with dust and debris.

Parker peered through the smoke and rubble,

searching for Alan. The man's face was a study of contrasts, his skin pale and bloodied from the flying glass. More blood flowed from his lower leg, pooling on the slate floor. Parker called his name, having no idea if his voice worked or if the man could hear him.

Keeping Becca between him and the burning car, Parker moved toward Alan and tried to rouse him. He didn't respond and Parker couldn't find a pulse. The man was dead. Because of him. Alan had paid the ultimate price for Parker's screwups. The truth leveled him as effectively as the bomb flattened his SUV.

Becca's lips were moving, although he couldn't make out the words through his battered ears and torrent of guilt. Dumbfounded, he watched her reach out and close Alan's eyes.

"Parker!" she cried. Her smaller hands shoved at his shoulder. "What do we do?"

He heard her, barely. It didn't matter really. He didn't have an answer. Might as well let fate come to him.

She caught his face and forced him to meet her gaze, held him so close his nose brushed hers. "Parker. Help *me*. I don't know what to do."

It might have been the tremor in her hands, or the way she said his name, but something finally cut through the shock. He leaned forward and kissed her, fast and hard, startling them both.

"No sense dying with regrets." As a romantic gesture, it didn't qualify, though her lips tilted into a bewildered smile. It gave him the hope he needed.

Lurching to his feet, he said a quick prayer for Alan while his mind leaped into tactical mode. Everything had been in that vehicle. His go-bag, her suitcase, her electronics and his were ash. They were down to the cell phone in his pocket, the pistol in his ankle holster and the torn-up clothing they were wearing.

Outside, the SUV continued to burn. People were inching closer, cell phones held high as they took pictures and video of the flames dancing and smoke billowing up into the blue sky above. Still a bit dazed and half deaf, the coppery sting of blood in his mouth, he understood the fob must have triggered the explosion. He tossed it into the debris scattered across the floor. Maybe it would help the police.

The safe room upstairs beckoned, but he'd stripped it of anything that would help them now. Hiding up there while they waited for help meant putting more lives in the line of fire. And for what? This was his fight. "We have to get out of here." Any one of those bystander phones might already have caught a glimpse of them.

He drew her down the hallway, back toward the front door of the building, and checked for anyone keeping watch outside. He caught sight of a slender man with dark hair leaning against a parked car, smoking a cigarette. He bore a close resemblance to the sentry at the awards gala. While Parker watched, the man's gaze drifted lazily from the scene of the explosion, up to the roof and then down the block.

"Who is that?" Becca's breath whispered over his cheek.

"No idea," he replied. "I'm guessing he's not on our side." He ushered her away from the slash of light from the front lobby door, into the shadows of the stairwell.

Every second counted and each minute felt separated, standing apart from the minute before it, the minute that would follow. They had to move, to hide or they'd both be dead by the end of the day. Noticing the scratches on the backs of her hands and the small burns on her clothing, he was furious for his errors that had painted a target on her head. It had been a narrow miss.

"Do you trust me?"

"Yes." She put her hand in his and kept pace with him as they ran back upstairs.

At the top floor, he turned toward the service hallway and entered the code for the roof access. He paused long enough to send a text message to the office. The short sentence was a code for his assistant.

Though it was possible the assassin had managed to track him through his phone, it was a risk they had to take if they were going to get away.

He slid his phone into a pocket and zipped it shut. He eased open the door to the roof, relieved they weren't greeted by a shower of bullets, and closed it again quickly. Reaching for her, he tipped up her face to the faint light coming through the screen at the top of the door. He stroked his thumbs over her cheeks, wiping away the smudges and turning her face side to side. Other than the shallow scrapes along her jawline and under her ear, she looked all right.

"You can see okay, right?"

"Yes," she said, her auburn eyebrows knitting together over the wary gaze that seemed to be her default way of viewing the world. "Can you?"

He grinned. "I'm good. We're going straight out this door and over the edge. Fast as you can move. Stay low, don't stop and know I'll catch you."

"You can fly now?"

"I wish. There's a balcony. From there, we work our way out of the neighborhood." And eventually he'd get her out of the city and out of harm's way. It was an argument they could have later, assuming they survived the next few minutes. "Ready?"

"One second." She fisted her hands in the panels of his jacket and pulled him close. Her lips met his with an urgency that shot through his veins like a bolt of lightning.

He wrapped his arms around her, bringing her flush against his body. At last, he indulged the fantasy of claiming her mouth. Her lips parted and his tongue stroked across hers. The pleasure and heat wove a spell around him. He ran his hands up over her ribs, his thumbs following the soft curve of her breasts.

He was seeing fireworks behind his closed eyelids, but the sound track of heavy boots thundering on the stairs brought him slamming back to reality. Breaking the kiss, her taste lingering on his tongue, he pushed open the door and they ran.

He kept his body between her and the door, sheltering her until the last possible second. Surging around her, he went over the roof first. He heard her swear when he dropped out of sight and suppressed a chuckle. He liked her creative vocabulary.

Landing, he turned and looked up in time to watch her make the leap. Grit, determination and blind faith were a heady combination, he thought, catching her, letting her slide down his body until they were both safe on the balcony of the second-floor condo. "Nice job."

"Thanks. I dated a stuntman for a while," she said.

Part of his brain mulled that over with a foreign twitch of jealousy as he guided her to the balcony on the next building. From there he followed her down a large cypress tree as easily as descending a ladder. Hearing a loud crack, he looked up as a bullet tore through the branch he'd just left.

Glancing back to the rooftop of his building, he saw the man with the scar raise a rifle. Parker ducked around the trunk of the tree, covering Becca. Two more gunshots ripped through the air, biting into the tree trunk, followed by the welcome sound of emergency sirens.

BECCA, WRAPPED IN Parker's protective embrace, felt his body jerk and heard him groan while they waited out the shooter. "Are you hit?"

"He missed me."

She suspected a lie, but this wasn't the time to debate it. "Where to?" The tidy courtyard garden between the buildings seemed as big and open as a football field now that someone was shooting at them.

His embrace eased, his hands light on her shoulders as he squared her in the direction he wanted her to go. "Through the gate, over the fence and across the next street. I can borrow a van from the inn on the next block."

Borrow. She wondered about his definition. "All right."

"Run and don't look back."

She wasn't about to make that promise. "Then you'd better keep up, because I'm not leaving you behind."

Before he could argue, she grabbed his hand and used every ounce of the adrenaline coursing through her body—from that searing kiss and the outrageous danger—to get through the gate. Remembering her days on various movie sets, she released him just long enough to get over the fence. Hand in hand, they raced across the street and moved from one bit of cover to the next as they headed for the low-rise inn right on the ocean.

Although the bullets had stopped, Parker wasn't behaving as if the immediate threat was over. "What are you thinking?" she asked.

"Keep moving," he said, his voice tight. "We're almost safe."

She glanced up at his smudged face, relieved his eyes were alert when he met her gaze. She squeezed his hand, grateful he'd pulled himself away from the abyss that had nearly dragged him under when he saw Alan's body.

Becca promised herself she could vomit later. Not now when it could slow them down. "Your phone is ringing," she said when she heard the classic rock riff emanating from his pocket.

He waited to check it until they were safely inside

the rear lobby of the inn. He swore as a faint smile ghosted across his lips. "Change of plans."

She tried to get a peek at the screen, and got distracted by the blood on his hand. "You're hurt. How bad is it?"

"It'll wait," he said. "One more sprint and we're out of here. Can you do that?"

"No borrowed van?"

"We've been upgraded," he said with a bewildered expression.

She suspected running from an assassin didn't often go as planned, and this twist appeared to be in their favor. "I'm game if you are," she replied. "Lead the way."

She tucked herself under his injured arm as they walked out of the inn, marveling at how quickly opinions could change. This morning, she'd been willing to cause him any harm to get away. Now a part of her ached knowing he'd been hurt protecting her. When he'd asked her about trust, her affirmative answer was pure instinct. She'd made a gut call in the heat of the moment, but she knew when the dust settled the answer would be the same. Despite all the things she should still be furious about, she did trust him.

A nice bonus, considering she was already addicted to his hot, possessive kisses.

She noticed the wince of pain when he broke into a jog as they reached Golden Gate Park. "Are we still being followed?"

"Not for much longer." He pointed to the sky. "Hear that?"

It took her a second to realize it was a helicopter rotor. "That's our upgrade?"

He nodded, taking her hand again as they ran toward the sound. They reached the soccer fields, and a moment later the small helicopter with the Gray Box logo set down long enough for them to climb on board. When they were buckled in, the pilot lifted off and circled, getting to altitude.

Becca watched, more than a little awed at the views of the city flowing by below. "Where are we going?" she asked.

"I'm not sure," he replied. "Sam Bellemere seems to have hijacked my escape plan."

"That's what happens when you hang with billionaires," she said.

"Rush and Sam were outcasts when we were in high school." He brought her hand to his lips for a moment. "Thanks for sticking with me." He loosened his grip on her hand, making it clear that any continued contact was her choice.

Lacing her fingers with his, she connected the dots between what he'd said and left unsaid. She knew a bit about Rush from her interviews. Although some of his competitors had labeled him and his partner as cocky, she'd always found he could back up even the biggest claims. "Those two were your investment strategy?"

Parker gave a nod, his gaze locked on the view through the windscreen. "I didn't have anything better to do with the money when it landed in my lap." He shrugged a shoulder. "They needed investors. It worked out for everyone."

"You don't need to be ashamed of being wealthy," she said, earning his full attention.

"I'm not." His brown eyes were filled with emotion, his lips pressed into a flat line. "I should've paid the ransom."

"No." The man was hurting, not just from the wound in his arm, and she wanted to make it better. "You said it yourself. If the blackmailer wanted money, we wouldn't be here."

"At least not until next week." His laughter was bitter and weak.

"Don't start second-guessing now, Parker," she said in the tone she used with unruly reporters. "Your car didn't explode from a random malfunction. It certainly wasn't a typical act of terrorism." They both knew terrorists wouldn't risk exposure and criminal charges over such a low potential casualty count. "This was personal."

"That's what scares me," Parker admitted.

She could already see where this conversation was headed. He wanted to send her away. Fortunately for him, the argument would have to wait as the helicopter began its descent over a building in the heart of the city.

Chapter Nine

Parker's gaze drifted around the sparsely furnished condo and he thought billionaire lessons might be a good idea. Sam and Rush had conspired to keep an eye on him after his visit to Gray Box yesterday. Parker hadn't considered the idea that doing research from a location protected from prying eyes might have prying eyes on the inside.

Not that he wasn't grateful for the assist.

Sam had tapped into his cell phone GPS and kept a police band open. Parker had only made it easier when he called for help identifying the driver tailing him. When the emergency crews were dispatched to a fire near Parker's location, Sam had leaped into action, reorganizing Parker's most trusted team and sending the helicopter to bring them to the building Sam had purchased, stripped down and rebuilt per his exacting specifications.

While Parker was relieved to know he and Becca

were completely off the radar, guilt gnawed at him. There were three men on a list with targets on their backs. Tony hadn't checked in since following the burglar from Becca's apartment, and Alan was dead. For a security expert with a military background, Parker was doing a lousy job of keeping people safe.

He replayed the explosion over and over, looking for the next step forward, while he showered off the smoke and debris and let the doctor Rush had sent over treat the wounds in his shoulder and leg. The assassin's bullets had missed him, but not the splinters from the tree. Parker turned down the offer of painkillers, wanting to keep his head clear.

Recognizing his primary mistake, he wished he could go back for a do-over. It was as if his military background had fallen out of his head. He'd slipped into the civilian tendency to underestimate an opponent. Cocky and overconfident, he'd relied too much on his home field advantage. The world was a smaller place in recent years and it was too easy for people to travel and train with experts anywhere around the globe.

The man—or men—hunting him and his team were definitely in the top of their class.

He'd seen it in those eyes when the man had the syringe to Becca's neck. Recalling those first images of her coughing and sputtering from the smoke, tears rolling down her soot-smudged cheeks from red-rimmed eyes, he swore. He'd nearly gotten her killed too.

"Are you hurting?"

He turned at the sound of Becca's voice and tried to dredge up a smile despite the guilt weighing him down. "I'm fine."

Her blue eyes searched his face and he knew she saw the lie. He waited for her to call him on it. She didn't. She crossed the room and wrapped her arms around him in a gentle hug that felt like a cool balm, soothing him from head to toe.

She'd been seen by the doctor and given a chance to shower and change as well. He breathed in the fresh clean scent of her hair, appreciated every healthy inch of her in his arms. "You smell fantastic."

"Thanks. You too." She stepped back and grinned at him, turning in a circle. "What do you think?"

Sam had checked their sizes and had clothing delivered for both of them. Parker had pulled on jeans and a blue button-down shirt, while Becca had chosen black slacks that hugged her hips and an ivory cable-knit sweater. "You're gorgeous, Becca."

And he needed to get her far away from him to make sure she stayed that way.

"We should—"

"Go upstairs and thank Sam and Rush," she finished for him. "Lucy and Madison are bringing lunch." Catching his hand with hers, she tugged gently on his good arm, leading him closer to the elevator. "I'm not letting you overanalyze this alone."

"It's better to pick apart my mistakes as a group?" He knew he sounded like an ass and couldn't get a grip on the emotions slamming through him. The loss was bad enough, and the fear layered over all of it was paralyzing him. If another wrong move resulted in losing another friend, it would break him.

There had only been one other time in his life when he felt this overwhelmed, this uncertain of his ability to create a positive outcome.

She stopped at the doorway and laid her hand on his cheek. "Parker. Everyone upstairs is here to help."

"It's not their fight."

"It is now. This isn't the time to fall on your sword in a solo act of honor. You need your friends. *We* need them."

He arched an eyebrow. "We?" She couldn't mean it the way some part of him wanted her to mean it.

"If you didn't want me involved, you shouldn't have kept me locked up like a pet hamster in a cage."

"That's not what happened," he shot back.

"Facts are so often a matter of perspective," she said with a shrug. "Now you're stuck with me. Come on, they're waiting for us."

"Won't you please go visit family or friends? Preferably in Europe." His throat felt raw as he posed the question and he knew better than to blame it on the earlier explosion.

"No." She pursed her lips, linking her hand with his again. "Not without you." She walked out into the hallway, dragging him along, and pressed the button for the elevator.

"I've got a car downstairs," he said. Any woman who jumped off rooftops and dated stuntmen had to know how to handle a car like his Spyder. "Sam is storing it for me. You can take it anywhere you want." He told himself the offer didn't mean anything. He could buy another one any time he wanted.

"Not without you," she said again. She crooked her finger as she stepped into the elevator.

"Becca, be reasonable."

"That, I can do." She gave him a soft kiss, eased back as if gauging his reaction. "I can't seem to stop doing that," she mused. "Let's share a meal with friends and we'll both be reasonable."

Parker knew he'd been manipulated. He just couldn't work up much irritation over it. She was right. They needed the meal, the sense of normal conversation to push aside the last of the morning tension.

He'd never been up to Sam's home after it was complete, only to the garage and the computer lab, and on one emergency response to the lobby downstairs a few months ago. Until he met and married Madison, Sam had spent most of his time at the Gray Box offices.

It was a temporary reprieve and all six of them knew it. An outsider would probably think they were three happy couples gathered for a relaxing weekend. While happy might apply to Rush and Lucy and Sam and Madison, he and Becca needed a different descriptor.

By some tacit agreement, they kept the conversation on lighter topics while they made the most of the big sandwich platters and sides of potato salad, fruit and coleslaw Lucy and Madison had brought over.

As Lucy passed a plate of chocolate chunk cookies around, Sam broached the topic with an apology.

"Being such an introvert myself and so protective of our work, I thought it was hypocritical for me to poke into your searches, knowing you expected privacy," Sam said to Parker. Turning to Becca, he added, "I'm sorry."

"I'm grateful," she replied with a warm smile. "You were a huge help today. All of you."

"What are you going to do about it?" Rush asked Parker.

"Does everyone know the basics?" There was concern on each face around the table.

"I filled in a few missing pieces while the doctor was working on you," Becca said. "Resistance is futile," she added with a quick flash of that smile.

He kept expecting her to come to her senses and withdraw from him. She didn't, staying close, showering him with inexplicable affection. Yes, they'd come through a harrowing morning, but he'd treated her poorly since rescuing her from the gala.

Parker pulled out his phone and shared his latest efforts. "No word yet on the favor I called in at Homeland on the man with the scar. I thought it would help to know how he got into the country."

"I can follow up," Madison offered. "Maybe a call from the State Department will light a few more fires. Do you think he is Iranian?"

"I'm ninety-nine percent sure the person paying his way is." He pulled up the pictures and handed her the cell phone. "Becca did sketches. I haven't had a chance to send them out for facial recognition."

"I can help with that too," Sam said. "We might find a trail of where he's been around the city."

While Parker's phone made the circuit around the table, he explained how he'd also sent reinforcements to help watch the backs of the other men on the list.

Becca swiveled in her seat to face him, her knee bumping his. "You have offices in other cities?"

"No. I made calls," he said. "Traded a few favors among colleagues."

Her auburn eyebrows gathered in a thoughtful pucker over her freckled nose, but she didn't say any more. He knew that look meant her mind was working overtime. Maybe she'd finally come to her senses.

"I appreciate what you've all done." This had been one of the toughest briefings of his life. Admitting his faults to clients who trusted him with their security wasn't the way to keep them on board. "Staying here puts you in jeopardy." He caught a speaking glance between Sam and Madison. "If you can help Becca get somewhere safe, I'll send a protective detail with her."

"No," Becca said flatly. "We still need to speak with the police."

His first instinct was to forbid her to leave Sam's building until he took care of the assassin. As the words danced on the tip of his tongue, he realized how ridiculous such an order would sound. That didn't even factor the uselessness of it. He could practically hear her laughing in his face. When she made a decision, she stuck with it. He just couldn't figure out why she was sticking by him after what he'd done.

"We can invite Detective Baird here," Lucy suggested.

"Or send you to his station by helicopter," Rush added.

Parker gave a snort. "By now, the team after us has probably acquired surface-to-air missiles."

"If you want to give a police statement, I can arrange that from the lab downstairs," Sam said. "You can do phone, video or secure instant messaging. Whatever you prefer."

"Baird would prefer face-to-face," Parker murmured.

He would prefer to get Becca out of the way and set a trap for the man hunting his team. He'd assisted in the security design here. Sam's building might as well be a fortress between the physical and technological barriers. They could hide in this building indefinitely, or until Sam's generous hospitality wore out. Parker's skin crawled at the thought of being trapped, being dependent on others to bring in supplies.

The irony of it, considering he'd done the same thing with less explanation to Becca, put a knot in his stomach. He stood up, distancing himself from the group to stare through the floor-to-ceiling windows. He couldn't enjoy Sam's superb panoramic view.

Someone was down there wreaking havoc on his team, on the city, on innocent bystanders.

"I still haven't heard from Tony," he said abruptly. "Set it up so both Becca and I can check in with the police and we'll go from there."

"On it," Sam said.

A few minutes later, while the others were chatting, Becca joined him at the window. "You have good friends," she said softly.

"They are." In a terrifying flash he saw them all dead, the scarred man standing over the bodies, sneering at him. Similar artificial scenarios had bothered him in the past, usually before a mission. It wasn't foresight, just the brutal awareness of how quickly a plan could go awry.

He turned to look at her. "I considered asking you to stay put until the threat is contained."

Her lips twitched. "And you've reconsidered, I hope?"

"Would you leave town?" he asked hopefully. "Think of it as a vacation."

She reached out and smoothed the shirtsleeve at his shoulder. "You're kind of cute when you're trying *not* to be a dictator."

"Could I convince you to cooperate with a twenty-four seven protective detail?"

"Only if you're on it," she replied breezily.

He'd never met a woman who could flirt over life and death. If this was flirting. Maybe she had a thing for the bad-boy types. He had a laundry list of credentials to back up that label. "Why are you here?"

She lifted those big blue eyes, holding his gaze, but before she could answer, Sam called up from the lab, "We're ready to roll."

WHY ARE YOU still here? His question and how she could best answer it swirled in the back of Becca's mind as they went down to Sam's isolated computer lab. The obvious reply was that she could see Parker faltering under the weight of his burdens and she wanted to help. He was compounding his grief by stifling it. She knew because she'd seen a similar expression in the mirror after her mother died and her father pushed her away a little more each year.

Alone wasn't an ideal way to get through life. Sinking into work and calling it thriving in order to avoid personal attachments wasn't the answer either.

Lucy and Madison had cornered her as soon as the doctor had examined her, vowing to have their husbands help them have Parker drawn and quartered if he'd done something out of character and hurt her. He hadn't, she assured them. He'd confused her, infuriated her and saved her life more than once. Through it all, he hadn't hurt her.

Yet. She kept that to herself.

Deep down, she knew he could. Not physically, never that, but emotionally. Although that should scare her, she couldn't seem to stop moving toward him. She recognized attraction and lust well enough. She knew she had adrenaline-junkie tendencies, and the last few days had tested that facet of her personality. This was different. Parker signified something far more dangerous than all that.

Why are you still here? It was only a matter of time before she had to answer that—for both of them. She hoped courage wouldn't fail her.

They were seated together at one of Sam's workstations, and after the brief introductions, Detective Baird aimed most of his questions at Parker, starting with his statement on the explosion. He wasn't happy they'd fled the scene, but he was very interested in Parker's take on the details.

"I left the key fob behind," Parker was saying.

She hadn't seen him do that.

"The thing went up like a Roman candle when I hit the remote starter."

Baird scowled as he made notes. "This guy wasn't expecting that."

"No. Early detonation saved us."

While he explained Alan's injuries, she shifted, rubbing his knee with hers so her support wasn't too obvious.

She appreciated that Parker kept up the reassuring knee-to-knee contact as she gave her account of the morning's events.

"Anything else you'd care to add, Mr. Lawton?"

"I was aware they were tracking the car," Parker

said. "I'd planned to go straight from the condo to the police station."

She bit back the interruption. The tracking detail was news to her.

"They must have set the bomb while I was inside with Ms. Wallace. Since Theo's murder I regularly scan my car for threats. It was clean a few hours prior."

Detective Baird turned his focus on her. "Can you explain why you were staying there rather than your home?"

She felt Parker tense up. Years of living and working with her father had honed her ability to deliver a role convincingly. Clearly he expected her to tell the detective she'd been kidnapped and locked in the safe room. "Mr. Lawton was concerned for me after I was attacked at the awards gala on Thursday night. He suggested I might want to take a break from my routine and generously offered me the space. Since he's the expert, I took his advice."

He arched an eyebrow, clearly skeptical. "You didn't report the attack." Baird shifted his attention to Parker. "Neither did you, Mr. Lawton, when we spoke on Friday."

"There was no evidence linking her attack and Theo's murder," Parker replied flatly. "I was just in the right place at the right time."

"Uh-huh. And now?"

"It would seem the two events may be connected after all," he admitted. "There was a second man serving as a lookout when Miss Wallace was attacked at the hotel. I believe he was also observing the scene at the explosion."

"I tend to draw the way other people journal," Becca volunteered, as Parker's jaw tensed. "I have sketches of the man with the scar and a profile of the other man."

They gave Baird a description of both men and Parker sent him an email with the picture of her sketches as well.

Parker leaned closer, draping his arm across the back of her chair, his fingers stroking her shoulder in a soothing motion. The detective narrowed his gaze at the protective gesture. "Have you made any progress on Theo's case?" Parker asked.

"No. We'll canvass the area again with this picture," Baird promised. "Has the brother called you?"

Parker shook his head.

"We expect to release the body later today. I got the feeling he wanted to discuss final arrangements with you."

"I'll keep my phone on," he promised.

"The Northern Police Station has been trying to reach you, Miss Wallace."

"My phone was in the SUV," she said, well aware that didn't account for the hours before the explosion. "I haven't had time to replace it. What was the trouble?"

The detective made a note and continued. "A bystander reported a burglary in progress at your address last night. Someone broke your window and searched your apartment."

She trembled at the idea, imagining what might have happened if she hadn't been in Parker's safe room. "Did they take anything?"

"Best we can tell, the obvious targets of electronics and personal valuables were ignored, but only you will know for sure. It's possible the bystander's call interrupted the burglar's plan. You'll need to schedule a walk-through with the officer on that case."

"Of course," she replied with a tight smile. "It will be my next call." She didn't want to go anywhere near her apartment without Parker. The police were more than capable in most circumstances, though she didn't know how they'd hold up if the assassination team from Iran showed.

"Is there any way to speak with the bystander who called it in? I'm sure Becca would like to thank him."

She smiled on cue, struggled to hold the expression as the detective scrubbed at his jaw. The man was stalling, debating what to share with them.

"We don't know for sure who called it in," Baird said, toying with the pen in his hands. His gaze shifted from her face to Parker's. "There's another matter I'm not sure is related. The unit that responded to the burglary call stumbled across a body a block from the scene during their search. No ID on him."

Parker's arm stiffened behind her shoulders. "You think the dead body is related to the burglary simply because of proximity?"

"We have to keep that in mind as we investigate."

Becca waited, her heart thudding against her rib cage.

"And?" Parker prompted.

"It caught my attention that the man they found in Russian Hill last night was killed in the same manner as Theo Manning. Two small-caliber bullets in the back of his head."

Becca pressed her fingers to her lips.

"Description?" Parker asked through clenched teeth.

Baird held up a picture of the man's face to the camera.

Parker swore under his breath. "That's Tony. He was in the area because I asked him to keep an eye on her apartment after the attack. I'll have my office send over his information."

Baird added more notes, then lifted his head and

glared at them. "Come clean with me, Lawton. You know something. How are these crimes connected?"

Becca turned as Parker did and they stared at each other a moment. Silently, she asked the obvious question with a slight tilt of her head. He gave her a reluctant nod. "Detective Baird, I may know a possible common denominator."

Surprise flowed over Baird's career-worn face and he leaned back a bit in his chair. "I'm all ears."

"Parker told me yesterday when and where Theo Manning died," she began. While she explained the email from the anonymous source and how she and Bill had proceeded, Parker grew more and more edgy. She made every effort to make it clear she didn't credit the claims against Parker or the other men, but he didn't relax. Not that she blamed him after the losses he'd suffered personally and professionally over recent days.

She didn't bring up the blackmail note—that was his decision. She also neatly avoided any mention of his visits to her apartment before and after the gala. Still, Parker was wound so tight she wondered when he'd snap.

"I'll need to see that email, Miss Wallace."

"Of course. We'll send it over right away."

When the call ended, Parker moved with silent, slow deliberation as he closed the camera and conference call applications. His lips were pressed into a thin line, and the dark circles under his eyes were more pronounced in his pale face. He'd lost another friend, and she ached for him.

"We'll send the email and Tony's details from another computer," he said. Taking no chances, he shut down the computer.

"Already done," Sam replied. "Seemed more expedient."

Parker gave him a short nod and stalked out of the lab.

"Thanks for all your help." Becca's relief that the conversation with the police was over was short-lived. She didn't know how to reach Parker, or if she should try. "I guess I'll go upstairs."

"Would you like to stay with us?" Sam asked. "Or I can open up another apartment. Just because you showed up together doesn't mean you have to stay there."

"Did you furnish all of them?"

"Four," he said sheepishly. "A friend needed the design practice."

"Lucy called him a stand-up guy," Becca said absently.

"He is," Sam agreed.

"That wasn't my first impression, in person," she admitted.

"And your second impression?"

"Different." Becca rubbed her arms, remembering those moments with Parker in the dark, as a delighted shiver skated over her skin. She'd been angry as his captive, but only her doubts about his identity had given her a reason to be afraid. "I'll go talk with him, if he'll let me."

"Make him listen," Sam suggested quietly as she reached the door.

Regardless of Parker's interpretation of the circumstances, he needed her. She couldn't leave him to brood about it too long, or they'd be back to square one with him pushing her away. The man had generously shared his resources and friends and even called in favors to protect her.

It was time he accepted what an asset she could be in the task of protecting him and the men on that list.

Chapter Ten

Becca walked into the apartment and found him in the kitchen slamming down a beer. Someone had stocked the refrigerator and brought in a basket of snacks while they were hashing things out with the detective. Parker wanted his own place, his own *space*. He just didn't trust himself to get there quite yet. He was too angry. He'd rather head down to his cabin in Big Sur. No one would pester him there.

Except a nasty, scar-faced assassin.

That was what he wanted, what they all needed. He should lead the bastard away, finish it one-on-one where he couldn't murder any more innocent people.

Might not win that fight, said a pesky little voice in his head. If he lost, would Jeff and Franklin and Matt and Ray really be safe? He slid a glance at the woman sitting at the counter, contemplating the snacks. Would she be safe?

"You know Sam has stronger stuff upstairs," she said, catching him watching her.

"I need to be alone," he snapped. He needed to think about how to reel this guy in close enough to finish him off.

"All right." She gave him plenty of room as she went to the couch and sat down.

He set his beer aside and went after her, perching on the coffee table in front of the couch. "Why didn't you tell Baird I kidnapped you?" He wanted an answer. Nothing about her made any sense to him. He wanted to drink her in, from the rich red silk of her hair to the creamy tips of her toes. He jerked his gaze away. It was official. He'd finally lost his mind.

"Because it was a rescue."

"I should have let you go right away." He paced away from her. "I wasn't thinking."

"Grief makes us do strange things. I'm over the awkward start, Parker. Are you?"

He stared at her. Was she that generous or that foolish? "You need to get away from me." Begging went against his nature, but he'd do it to spare her from the looming battle. This was too serious. A team of assassins had targeted him for things he'd done in a remote area on the other side of the world. Twelve people had died over there. Three people were dead here—so far. She'd nearly joined that inexcusable statistic.

Even if they got around the man with the scar and his pal, that didn't mean it was over. There might be someone else later who would be even more ruthless. He had to make her see reason.

Think first. He raked his hand through his hair. If only he had taken time to think first, she might be on a second date with the weasel-faced man who'd taken her to the awards gala. *Or at the mercy of the man with the scar*, a cruel voice in his head added.

"Parker."

When she squeezed his hands he dragged his attention away from the charred wreckage of his thoughts to study her face. "You have to get out of here, Becca. Out of the state, if possible. You have to see how dangerous it is to be around me."

"On the contrary," she said, massaging his hands. "You keep proving how adept you are at keeping me safe." She lifted those clear blue eyes to his. "Even when I didn't know I needed it."

He tried again. "This is my fight. My problem." If they'd done the job right the first time, there wouldn't have been anyone left to come after them.

Her jaw set into a stubborn line and her eyes sparked. "It may have started that way, but—"

"No buts." *You're too important to me.* He managed to keep those words tucked away where they couldn't create more trouble. "You need to get out of the cross fire." How could she overlook the obvious fact that sooner or later people got hurt around him?

If she got hurt, or worse, he'd never forgive himself. She wasn't an innocent bystander, some faceless collateral damage in a godforsaken war zone. He'd come to care about her, though none of his actions could remotely be interpreted in such a positive or benevolent way.

"It's too late for that. You can't finish this alone, Parker."

He wrenched his hands from her grasp and stalked back to the kitchen.

"How about this?" she said, following him. "I'll leave town when you do. After."

"After what?" he asked.

She drilled a finger into his chest. "After you."

"Of all the stupid criteria…" He stopped when temper flashed over her face. He rolled his shoulders back. She needed to accept the facts. "It may surprise you to hear you're not in charge, Rebecca."

Her eyes went wide. Her lips twitched and suddenly that remarkable laughter tumbled out of her, spilling over him. "It might not have shown up in a background check," she said, mimicking his dry tone, "but that's never stopped me before."

He sidled away as she leaned close. Touching her would be a mistake to pile on to all the others he'd made with her. He crossed the room, putting the couch between them and praying for the ache in his gut to go away. It *was* too late. He was addicted to her already. The best solution was to cut himself off cold turkey.

He stuffed his hands into his pockets. "I'll take you to LA," he said.

"That's not a bad idea," she said thoughtfully. "My dad is away and we can stay at his place in Malibu."

"Stop being difficult." He clenched his jaw, searching for the patience he'd been praised for during the most grueling covert operations. "*You* can stay in Malibu while I finish business with the guy hunting my team."

Her gaze narrowed on him. "You're thinking of paying him off?"

"It's not so absurd." He had more than enough money.

"You said it yourself! It's not about the money," she shouted. She picked up a pillow and threw it at him. "What if—and I'm just brainstorming here—what if we worked on ending this *together*? There's Sam and Rush, Detective Baird, Madison and her contacts in the State Department. You might have noticed, I'm not without skills."

His shoulders locked as he turned away. Why wouldn't she leave him? "This is a mess from *my* past. You're only peripherally involved."

"Ohh."

He spun around, glaring at the way she dragged out that single syllable. "What does that mean?"

She hitched a shoulder. "It means this makes sense. You're wanting to do the whole martyr thing."

He stared at her.

"Is *penance* a better word for you?" she asked sweetly.

"Becca." Her name was little more than a growl. Too bad she wasn't easily cowed. "I'm done arguing." He caught her elbow and steered her toward the door. "Be smart and go up there and tell them you want to leave." Her escape window was quickly closing. As soon as the assassin learned where they were hiding, it would be a tougher task to get her out safely.

"I'm not leaving," she snapped. "And I have some ideas."

"Fine. Let's hear them." He let her have her say uninterrupted, listening with half an ear as he worked out the next steps. She could argue while he focused on getting both of them out of this alive. A plan was taking shape in his head while she tried to convince him she could be helpful.

He had the money and connections to buy a new

identification and background for her, but that took time. Although he barely knew her, he figured once her father learned of her disappearance, the man would move heaven and earth to find her.

She was equally valued at her network. They too would search for her if she just went off the radar. Plus, she loved her job and was good at it. A new identity meant no-turning-back changes he didn't want her to suffer. He had to solve this in a way that didn't leave her career in shambles.

"You're not listening," she said abruptly.

"I am," he protested.

She folded her arms and dared him with a raised eyebrow to tell her what she'd just said.

"A memorial service," he said. He'd heard that much. Studying her face, he tried to sort out how that would work.

"Oh, give up." She put her hands on his shoulders. "I suggested we stage a memorial service for Theo and invite the other men on your team."

"Are you crazy? It would be shooting fish in a barrel for the assassin if we were all in one place."

"I said *stage*," she said patiently. "I know plenty of actors in the area. You might have heard I have some experience with putting on a good show."

He caught himself before voicing his doubt about her idea.

"I don't mind that you don't believe me yet," she said with a serenity that put him on edge.

"You don't?"

Her lips curved into a sassy grin that lit a fire in his system and left him wondering why he'd limited their previous interactions to darkness. "Your disbelief doesn't make it less true."

He pondered that statement as he paced in front of the windows. "I considered a trap," he said.

"Great minds think alike," she said confidently. "Setting a trap with backup in place is a better idea."

"How would we be sure the assassin takes the bait?"

"Why don't we go ask Sam for advice on that?"

The smile that curved her lips had a sharp edge that made him thankful she was on his side. He just wasn't sure he could hang on to that hope when he didn't understand why she didn't leave him to deal with the mess on his own. Admittedly, his brain was muddled from grief and guilt. Maybe he was missing an important detail. Was she really willing to help? "One second," he said, catching her hand, needing the contact. "Becca, why are you still here?"

"You don't think I should be?" Her gaze dropped to their joined hands.

He reached out and tipped up her chin until he could see the flicker of nerves and excitement in her eyes. Her teeth bit into her lower lip as she stared at his mouth.

His body reacted predictably, going hard in an instant. "I want you, Becca."

She slid her tongue across her lips. "It's mutual, Parker."

The husky confession threw his lust into over-drive. He was no saint, just a man who knew how fleeting life could be. He crushed her mouth under his. Tasting and taking, letting her do the same. Her lips were soft and her response firm and willing as she met him move for move. Slipping his hands over the glorious curve of her hips, he pulled her close. Leaving no doubt about his need or intentions.

She rocked against him and moaned, winding her arms around his neck to press closer. Her fingernails grazed the edge of his ear, up into his hair, and he nearly lost it.

He pushed a hand up under her sweater. Her warm and supple skin rippled under his fingers. "Ticklish?" he asked, peppering kisses along her cheek and jaw.

"Maybe."

He tested the theory, drawing a helpless giggle out of her as she squirmed away and then closer. Something they could explore later. Right now he wanted her, wanted to bury himself deep inside her and forget everything but her.

He slid her sweater up and over her head, tossing it aside and guiding her back toward the couch. She stretched out and pulled him close. Her bra was black satin, cool and dark against her lovely, ivory skin. She worked open the buttons of his shirt and he'd never felt anything as wonderful as her palms running up and down his chest.

She pulled his mouth back to hers, her tongue tangling with his, and her hands seemed to be everywhere. His body reveled in her affection, even as he struggled to slow things down for their mutual pleasure.

Life offered no guarantees, and if this was the only chance he had with her, he wanted to make it unforgettable. She had his jeans open and her hand glided over him. He bucked at the touch, craving more.

He blazed a trail with his mouth down the column of her throat, dipping his tongue under the edge of her bra, then suckling her through the fabric. She cried out his name, arching into him and holding his head close.

He heard chimes and counted it a new high until Becca pushed at his shoulders. "Your phone," she said, pointing to where it had fallen on the floor.

"It's Sam." He sat up to answer the call, his eyes

cruising over Becca's luscious body. Unless the building was under attack, this wasn't over.

"Parker, we've got company. You guys need to come upstairs."

He immediately snapped back to business mode. "We're on our way." He ended the call and leaned over her, giving her a scorching kiss. "To be continued," he said, meaning it. He stood and helped her up.

"What's wrong?" The question was muffled as she pulled the sweater over her head.

"We've been found sooner than expected."

"Iran has a new enemy," she grumbled as they walked out.

"Then my money is on us." He laughed, reveling in the wonderful, normal feeling of holding her sweet, shapely body close to his on the brief elevator ride down to Sam's lab.

He hoped what they'd been doing wasn't too obvious to Sam and Rush when they walked into the lab. He shouldn't have worried. His friends were studying a monitor array with four views outside the building. Two more monitors showed Sam's open searches and a list of names.

Parker instantly locked on to the white sedan. "He's still using Jenny Swanson's car?"

"Looks like," Sam replied. "The beard is gone, but he hasn't changed the license plate."

Parker puffed out his cheeks and rocked back on his heels. "Send the cops out to her residence."

Becca gave his hand a gentle squeeze and he saw the comprehension in her gaze.

Sam opened an email window and sent the message along with still-capture pictures from the current surveillance feed, as well as the earlier shots from traffic cameras around the city.

"Should we invite Detective Baird over for dinner?" Rush asked.

"Becca came up with a different idea." He explained the concept of a fake memorial service for Theo, staged for the sole purpose of capturing the assassin and his partner staking out the building.

He let her explain how she planned to get actors to play the role of the other men on the list. "We would need to fake the travel records and credit cards," she added, layering in more details.

Uneasy, Parker amended her plan. "I'm not comfortable putting innocent people in this guy's sights. Let's assemble the team from my own crew and local experts."

Sam nodded. "We can do that."

Becca gave him a warm smile. "Parker said the

two of you would have come up with some idea to be sure the assassin takes the bait."

"He's sitting right there," Rush said, scowling at the monitor. "We could just go down and tell him."

"Whatever we do, I want Baird in on it," Parker said. "I want this guy to go down the right way." Theo, Jeff, Alan and Tony deserved justice more than revenge.

"Since your SUV blew up, I've been working to get an ID," Sam said. "Anything the police can use to haul this guy in."

Parker sensed a plan brewing. "What's on your mind?"

Sam was locked in to something. "There are two of them out there in one car." He zoomed in so they could all see. "How do you feel about a wild-goose chase?"

"I like it," Becca answered, her eyes bright.

"They're parked where they can see the garage entrance. Rush and I have a fleet and drivers who can meet us around front. All of us leave at the same time, head different directions."

Parker shook his head. "I won't take a chance on them hurting any of you or your employees."

"So we modify it," Becca said, touching his arm. "You and I leave, from the garage. Let them tail us."

"He must be monitoring you through the cell

phone GPS now. I can add text messages that allude to a small private service tomorrow evening. Gives the others time to travel."

"Choose a location that gives him an easy point of attack and escape," Parker said. "We want him to be comfortable enough to take us all on."

"Right." Sam brought up overhead views of various funeral homes around the city. After a few minutes, he used a stylus to circle the area. "We can put the service right here. It gives the appearance of being convenient for his coworkers, and it's close to the airport too."

Parker stepped up, analyzed it. "Looks good." He picked up a notepad and pencil and wrote down a series of instructions, waited for Sam and Rush to read them through. Both men nodded in agreement.

"We'll go pack a bag," he said. Then they'd be as ready as they could be. "Let's get this goose chase started."

Becca grinned and slipped her hand into his.

Chapter Eleven

Becca watched the world fly by as Parker worked his way south along the Pacific Coast Highway. The scenery was gorgeous with the sun falling toward the ocean, and once they'd left the city behind, there were stretches of the road when it felt as if they were the last two people on the planet. "Have you decided how far we're running?" she asked when they stopped for gas.

"Maybe once I decide where to stash you next." At least the suggestion was delivered with a wink this time.

"That's rich," she said, laughing a little. "Please be over the loner thing. We need to be a team."

"We certainly have some unfinished business." The heated look he aimed at her did crazy things to her belly. She checked the phone Sam had given her, just to keep her hands off Parker.

"Any word?" he asked, his gaze on the road.

"Sam says he's still in the city."

"Good."

She didn't understand all the technical details as Sam developed an electronic net to track the men hunting them while Parker arranged a bait and switch with his company trucks. He'd had a driver pick them up at Sam's building, and another crew took his cell phone and became the target of the sedan's interest when they circled the funeral home that would host the fake memorial tomorrow night. Sam was keeping tabs on all the players so they would know if and when they had to move.

Parker had headed out of town, just in case the ploy hadn't worked, while the team pretending to be them had retreated to the hotel where the other members of the team were expected to stay after the memorial. Assuming the plan succeeded, Parker and Becca had the rest of the night to themselves.

It was exciting and terrifying all at once. She felt safe with Parker, even safer now that they had backup, yet the high stakes made her cautious. "Do you ever wonder why they grabbed me?"

Parker's expression sobered and she wished she could erase the question, except now that it was out there she wanted to hear his answer.

He finished with the gas pump and gave her a hard look through the open car window. "It has to be my fault," he said. "Somehow the scarred man was on my tail when I went by your apartment. I was an idiot and I'm—"

"Don't apologize again." Without Parker's intervention, she might be dead by now. "And he tossed my apartment for a lead?"

"Probably." Parker shrugged and hopped back into the truck. "A lead on either one of us, I'm betting. He didn't find me until I used my SUV. It's the only car registered in my name."

She looked around. "So, where to next?"

His expression was unreadable. "There's a great little place down the coast, if you're up for another hour on the road."

She was up for just about anything with him, and an hour later he pulled the truck off the road and parked in front of a wind-battered restaurant perched on the edge of the cliff. Below she could hear the surf crashing into the coast. The sound put a smile on her face, and when Parker took her hand, her heart melted.

Inside, the ambience was a throwback to a classic diner, including padded chairs and stools upholstered in cherry-red vinyl. Tables were arranged to make the most of the view, including a long L-shaped counter. "Can't you just see this place fifty years ago with a full soda fountain?"

Parker took the counter stool next to her, chuckling as she swiveled back and forth. "You having fun?"

"Yes, actually." Her stomach rumbled and they ordered burgers, milk shakes and a double order of loaded French fries as soon as the waitress came by.

He dragged his hand down her arm when they were alone. "If you could live anywhere, where would it be?"

"Where's that coming from?" She leaned back, startled by the curiosity in his gaze.

"I snooped through your life, remember? Your work has taken you all over the world. What have you enjoyed most?"

While they watched the ocean, she relayed some stories of working on her father's sets in the United States and abroad, traipsing merrily through the good memories, the awkward and absurd moments in other cultures and her time with the various people who made productions possible. "It's the same kind of fun with my reporters, just on a smaller scale."

"Your dad doesn't get that."

She understood it wasn't a question and still she felt the need to defend him. "My dad is busy."

"I've only traveled with the military. They give us culture training, and it helps, though not nearly as much as meeting people one-on-one," he said. "And traveling with pals isn't the same as traveling with someone important."

Was he implying she was important to him? It gave her a little shiver of happiness. She bounced a little on the seat, her stomach growling in anticipation as her strawberry milk shake arrived. "I want you to know I was suspicious of that email from the start," she said after she managed to get her first taste of the treat.

"Why?" He stirred his milk shake with his straw, eyeing her closely.

"Gut instinct. The family that was supposedly robbed of their fortune would never have reached out to *me* for help. A news story would have been too shameful." She handed him a napkin from the dispenser on the counter when their food arrived. "I still had to verify it."

"I understand," he said. "In your shoes, I would've taken a deeper look too. Sometimes my clients give me the problem in a way that paints them in a better light than it should."

His words lifted a weight off her shoulders she hadn't realized she'd been carrying. "Thank you," she murmured.

He spread mayonnaise and mustard on the bun and stacked up his burger. "Want my tomato?"

"You're kidding." She gawked at him. "That's a heritage beefsteak tomato."

"Is that important?"

"Have you ever had one?" He shook his head and she bit back the lecture. "Taste it. If you still want to give it up, I'll gladly take it off your hands."

He pulled the tomato aside and cut off a small bite. She watched the reactions play over his face as he went from skeptic to believer with just one taste.

"Remarkable."

"I know, right? Of course, you've just been spoiled for all tomatoes in your future."

"I think it's worth it," he said, stacking up his burger.

They ate for several minutes in a satisfied silence.

"While we were working in that area of Iraq, we worked with two of the sons of the family named in your email and the blackmail note," Parker said quietly. "They're good people. According to Jeff, the oldest son, Fadi, is the driver who ran him off that bridge."

"Not a chance," she said. "I know we weren't there long, but I'm pretty good at reading people. Everyone in that village was relieved, delighted and hopeful about the efforts of our armed forces."

"You thought I kidnapped you," he pointed out.

"Well, I was on drugs." She grabbed another

French fry from the platter between them. Anything to chase away the grim fog of those minutes. "Bill and I spoke with the oldest boys about coming to America, and they only wanted a better life where they were. I don't believe anyone in that family would sink to the lows we've experienced."

"I double-checked anyway and called in a favor to confirm that Fadi is still at home," Parker said. "We know the blackmail letter was a ruse." He pushed a hand through this hair, ruffling the thick waves. "I played right into their hands."

They both had. There was something he wasn't saying, and she wasn't sure how to ask in a way that he would answer. Parker Lawton was an enigma wrapped in secrets and sealed with tape stamped Privacy Line. Do Not Cross. To respect and honor that line meant walking away, leaving the mystery of him unsolved.

He kept asking why she was here and she had to admit wanting to know his story was part of the answer. Not for the show, but for her heart.

"You've done the right thing every step of the way."

He shook his head and hunched over the rest of his meal. She didn't push the issue further, letting them both eat and rest and fuel up for the events ahead. She suspected even a fake funeral would take its toll on him.

"You know what bugs me most about all this?" she asked when she finished her burger.

"I wouldn't hazard a guess," he said, his gaze on the ocean.

She nudged his knee with hers. "Why? Why now, why this method and why the six of you by name?"

"Important questions," he said. "There's only one reason I can think of, and even after everything that's happened it still seems implausible."

"Spit it out."

Parker pushed his empty glass and cleaned plate toward the back of the counter. "Not here." He balled up his paper napkin and dropped it on the plate. "Is there any hope of having you sit somewhere safe until we spring the trap tomorrow?"

"No." She mimicked his move with her napkin. "We're in this together, Parker. Surely you've noticed I'm not a fragile, porcelain doll. You're stuck with me."

"Becca." He dropped cash on the counter to cover the meal and tip. "A ruthless, creative killer believes his targets will all be in one room tomorrow evening. There's dedication to a cause and loyalty to friends, and then there's insanity."

She studied his face, and although he didn't move,

she sensed he wanted to fidget. She covered his hand with hers. "I was willing to call in my actor contacts for this." Although she felt confident her contacts could have managed the ruse with his team working behind the scenes, she was grateful he'd assembled the stand-ins. It was progress for him. "I wouldn't have offered if I didn't believe the good guys will prevail."

"I appreciate all the positive thinking."

"You do not." She stood up. "I grew up in Hollywood. I know how to set a stage, create illusion and see through a smoke screen." Parker was blowing all kinds of smoke. She just didn't know why.

"And I know how to set security."

She bit back her assessment that his constant worry for her safety was stemming from misplaced guilt as much as good reason. If he heard her at all, he'd hear pity, which wasn't the point she was trying to make. "Do you want to take a walk on the beach before we head back?" she asked when they reached the truck.

"Sure." He guided her out of the restaurant with the whisper of a touch on her back.

She wanted to lean in or touch him in return. As he'd said, they had unfinished business. She couldn't forget the feel of his mouth and hands on her skin.

Her body hadn't really stopped humming since Sam interrupted them.

Well, we have the evening to ourselves, barring a surprise attack, she thought as they took the stairs carved into the cliff down to the crescent of a beach. She intended to put it to good use.

They sat on a rock and he drew her close, keeping her warm as they watched the ocean swallow the last rays of the sun. In that lovely, quiet twilight, as the first stars winked on in the velvety sky, she brought his hand to her lips and kissed his palm, then curled his fingers around it.

Back in the truck, she wondered if he'd ever opened up to anyone. He dealt in secrets for a living. Who was his confidant, his release valve? She shouldn't press him for how those six men from different units came to be on one list assembled by an assassin. If asked, he would surely prefer that she leave it alone, but she would regret it for him.

That was the crux of it, she realized. Parker might have everything in place on the surface, yet underneath, a part of him was lost. She recognized it because it had happened to her. The solution required someone to point it out and then a conscious choice to change.

She was more than a little surprised that the place he had in mind for the night was a courtyard of individual log cabins a couple miles inland from the diner. Although it didn't look like much on the outside, it was off the beaten path and they had an opening for the night. Inside the room, she was startled to see all the amenities of a five-star hotel, complete with a stocked mini fridge, a microwave and a king-size bed topped with pillows and fluffy white linens. "How did you discover this place?"

"A client," he said. "Referral from Rush, actually. We worked out a new surveillance system that doesn't go off every time a raccoon wanders across a porch. I come out once or twice a year just to clear my head."

"It's so unexpected," she said, trailing her fingertips over the smooth linen.

He sat down and started unlacing his boots. "I can order wine if you want. They have a good cellar."

"Really?"

He slid a look at her and she felt a blush stain her cheeks. They had the whole night ahead of them, and suddenly she was shy. "I'm good." Ignoring her surging hormones, she grabbed her overnight bag and headed for the bathroom to freshen up after the beach. At the last second, she decided to change clothes too.

In a T-shirt and comfy leggings, her hair brushed smooth, she stared into the mirror. Until Parker wanted to open up about his enemies, maybe they shouldn't take this further. Her body protested the idea and she sighed. Together they were combustible, that much was clear. She should just enjoy whatever they could share in the moment.

Her concerted efforts at personal life planning had fallen flat. She could hardly expect him to open up while she stayed safely in her shell. She walked out of the bathroom, determined to clear up a few misconceptions. "Parker—"

Her mouth went dry. He'd moved the chair around and his feet were bare, propped up on the edge of the bed, his laptop balanced on his thighs. Inwardly, she groaned. She couldn't have designed a more drool-inducing scene for herself.

She knew how strong he was, knew what those muscles felt like in fighting mode, and she wanted to discover what he would feel like in more intimate, uninterrupted pursuits. This afternoon hadn't been nearly enough to satisfy her curiosity and desire for him.

"Where'd you get the laptop?" She perched on the far side of the bed, tucking one leg underneath her. "Stupid question. Sam gave it to you."

"No such thing as a stupid question." He looked up from the screen, and the scowl on his face vanished, giving way to an intense, hungry smile.

Her skin warmed under his gaze. "You found something?"

"I wasn't in a patient mood. This can wait."

"Tell me." She joined him when he waved her over. "My friend at Homeland hasn't found anything helpful about how the men entered the country. Madison, however, has made progress. And I called in another favor, so the hotel emailed me the security footage from Thursday night. They'd invited me to their office, but I convinced them to send it out."

"How many people owe you favors?"

He looked up at her, considering. "Several."

"It must be interesting work you do." The weak response annoyed her. She should tell him what it meant to her to see him go to such lengths for her as well as for his well-being. She'd forever be frustrated that her own father had never shown such willingness to help her with far more typical concerns.

He set the computer aside, giving her his full attention. "It's what I do. It's all I know."

Though she didn't believe that for a minute, she changed the subject quickly. "What did Madison come up with?"

"This." Parker adjusted the screen so she could view it easily. "Look familiar?"

"Maybe?" The man in the picture was much bigger and a bit older than the slim man they'd seen watching the fallout from the car bomb.

"I'm not surprised," Parker said. "He grabbed you so fast."

"There's no scar." She laid a hand on his solid shoulder and leaned a bit closer to the screen. "Makeup?"

"No." He went still beneath her touch. "This is Samir Abdullah before…" In a flurry of action, he closed the laptop and stood up.

Before what? She didn't ask, refused to push him. He had to choose to open up.

He didn't. He retreated to the small refrigerator and pulled out a bottle of water.

She scrolled through the pictures Madison had sent. In one, the man, before he was scarred, stood with his hand on the shoulder of a lanky boy, beaming as if he'd caught a prize fish. There was something familiar about the boy's face as well, though she couldn't put her finger on it.

"He was basically a tyrant king running the insurgents in the area where you met Fadi and his family," Parker said beside her. "With his identity confirmed, Sam notified the authorities. If we're lucky, they'll drop a net over him tonight."

"I'm sorry I mistook you for the bad guy," she said.

"I wasn't exactly the good guy, keeping you locked up."

"Keeping me safe." She turned to him and

smoothed a hand up the placket of his shirt, resting it lightly on his shoulder. "And *you* never smelled like onions."

Parker's lips twitched, but he didn't laugh. He cleared his throat and hooked his hands in his back pockets. "I should apologize."

"I believe you've done that already," she said, holding her ground, holding his gaze.

"Not for that, for not being truthful about the whys."

"It can wait." She hooked her finger in his shirt collar and tugged a little, until his lips were within reach. The kiss she gave him was light, a flirty invitation if he wanted to play.

He didn't even blink.

Releasing his shirt, she stepped back, racking her brain for the right words to sweep this awkward moment under the nearest carpet.

"Becca. I want you." His voice cracked on the words. "You shouldn't want me."

The pain in his voice sliced through her, and anger followed. "I can *want* whomever I like," she replied. "We might want each other, but I believe you need me as well. I'm not perfect and I don't expect you to be."

"Perfect?" He groaned. "I'm a killer," he said suddenly. "We were in the area, a task force sent to stop

Samir." He turned his back on her, and the story poured out of him in a rush that had his shoulders quaking. "The man had stolen children, among other heinous crimes. We shouldn't have been surprised he used the villagers as an escape strategy."

She wanted to comfort him, to erase the pain, and knew letting him share was the only way.

"Fighting amid the villagers, we couldn't call in a drone strike. It was all hand to hand, up close, personal and bloody as we cut down his group one by one. We cornered him and eventually chased him out of that village. Blew up his car as he made a run for the border. I don't know how he survived, or who helped him identify the six of us. God. There was so much blood and chaos."

"It sounds like hell."

"It was." He choked on the admission.

"And you survived." She moved to him, rubbing his back and then hugging him from behind, laying her cheek against the solid strength of his back. "You all came home and thrived."

"Hardly. He used me to find them, and is mowing us down in retaliation."

"Hush." She slipped around in front of him and cradled his face. "You did what had to be done, Parker, that's all. I'm so sorry for the price you've paid in the process."

She pressed up on her toes and kissed his lips. "We have a plan." She kissed his cheek. "We'll take care of him once and for all." Kissed the other cheek. "Together." She smiled, wondering if anything she said was sinking in. "Trust your friends and favors and resources."

He blinked away the sheen glistening in his dark eyes. "You're still here," he murmured, trapping her hands against his cheeks.

She nodded, not trusting her voice.

He reached over and turned off the floor lamp, throwing the room into darkness. A moment later, a thrill danced up her spine when his strong hands gripped her hips, pulled her flush against his muscled body. "Becca," he whispered against her lips.

She nipped his lower lip, clinging to his shoulders for balance as his kiss set her head spinning. She reveled in the heat, the velvet stroke of his tongue against hers. Under her hands she felt his breath stutter in and out. Good. She ran her hands over the hard planes of his chest and fumbled with the buttons of his shirt. Nothing would stop them this time.

As if he could see in the dark, his gripped her hips and boosted her up. She locked her legs around his trim waist as he carried her unerringly to the bed.

This. Yes. More. The world dwindled down to

the two of them. Nothing else existed, nothing was needed, beyond the delight and indulgence right here.

His fingers sank deep into her hair and he pulled just enough to bring her head back so he could feast on her throat. She shoved at his shirt and hers until at last they were skin to skin. His mouth traced her collarbone, then drifted lower, pressing kisses over her heart while he thumbed her nipples.

She cried out when his mouth closed over one taut peak and suckled hard. He broke contact and she whimpered until she heard the sound of his zipper lowering. She scrambled to get out of her leggings and panties and heard a thud as something hit the floor.

"What was that?" she said.

"Not important."

He was right. She reached for him, explored him in the darkness as he worshipped her with his mouth and hands, every wicked touch bringing her closer to the peak. She tasted the salt on his skin, inhaled the scent that was him alone, found the places that made him shudder.

She was begging, her body eager, when he spread her thighs and filled her. She nearly came at that first touch. He changed the angle, and pure pleasure flamed through her. Gripping his hips, she matched the rhythm as relentless and timeless as the ocean until she had to let go and surrender to the shattering climax.

Her body shivering around his, she could only hang on as he brought her to another peak before giving in to his own release.

They drifted there, in that starry bliss, with soft kisses and softer words.

When he drew her to his side and pulled up the comforter over their cooling bodies, she remembered the thud and the laptop he'd put on the bed. "I hope the computer's okay," she said with a giggle.

"Sam has more." His hand danced down her rib cage, tickling her.

On a glorious burst of laughter, she let him roll her over and start thrilling her again.

Chapter Twelve

Sunday, October 17

Parker woke to a spill of sunlight through the curtains, surprised to find he'd slept soundly for the first time in recent memory. As he felt the warm, seductive curves of Becca snug beside him, the reason for this bone-deep happiness filtered through him and left him smiling.

Everything about her tempted him, enticed him. She was brave, bright and sexy as hell. And for some reason he wasn't ready to label, he got a hollow feeling in his gut when he imagined going back to his life without her in his face, challenging him on every detail.

Before reality could intrude, they made good use of the oversize shower and the breakfast he'd ordered last night while she dozed.

As they drove back to San Francisco, they talked

more about Theo and the others, as well as her career path at the network. Not knowing what the evening would hold, or if she'd even want to stick around once the rush of their ordeal was over, he didn't want to jinx these priceless moments.

Sam had called before they set out, to let them know Samir was still locked on to the hotel where he thought Parker and Becca had spent the night, so they drove straight to Sam's building and a meeting with Detective Baird and Special Agent Spalding, an FBI connection of Madison's.

They reviewed every detail. "The only person who isn't a stand-in is Theo's brother David," Special Agent Spalding reported. "We couldn't convince him to stay out of it."

Parker glanced at Becca and caught her smirk. "I can sympathize," he said. "As long as he knows how to get out of the room, that's all we can do."

Just as Becca had assured him, the plan was in place and working. It was simply a matter of waiting for the right time to move in.

The countdown was running in the back of his mind as they gave their statements to the police and FBI and connected the dots on Samir, his revenge mission and the other man whom they believed to be a cousin of Fadi.

Finally, it was go-time and he could stop thinking

about the what-if and what-next questions. He had a target and he meant to hit it.

When they walked into the small chapel at the funeral home, Parker's brain kept flip-flopping about Becca at his side. He wanted her safely away from this potential nightmare, and yet if she were out of his sight, he knew he'd be distracted with worry. Samir had gone after her before. There was nothing to say he wouldn't try again.

She looked stunning in a quiet black dress with pearl earrings and a long strand of pearls that draped to her waist. He wanted to run his hands through her gorgeous auburn hair, remembering the feel of the silky waves against his skin.

"All clear, survey one." The voice in his ear brought him back to reality with a jolt. Surveillance one was stationed on the street out front. He and Becca, David and the crew posing as Theo's mourners were all in place. In the still, somber mood in the room, aware he'd have to do this for real if he survived, Parker found it hard to breathe. Without the distraction of the trap, he'd bolt for his cabin in Big Sur and work through this as God intended: alone with his thoughts and a bottle of whiskey.

Make a move, Samir, he thought. *Let's end this.*

"Relax," Becca said, slipping her hand over his arm. "It will be over soon."

"I want my target," he murmured for her ears alone.

"I understand." She leaned in just a bit. "The service will begin shortly."

He hadn't wanted to take the charade that far, but David insisted he could handle it, especially if it meant catching Theo's killer.

"You've set a good stage here," Parker said, trying to steel himself against the emotion threatening to swamp him.

"Thank you." She rubbed her hand up and down his arm.

He relaxed a fraction under the soothing touch. "The flowers are a nice touch."

Plants and floral arrangements had been placed about the room, all of them props that hid weapons. "Why doesn't the bastard make his move?" he asked after another round of check-ins sounded in his ear.

"You're antsy. It's understandable. Let's get started. Just to keep up appearances."

Parker nodded at David, who stepped to the podium near the closed casket. As David played his part, Parker calculated angles and choke points. They were dealing with two men, a leader and an accomplice or more likely an apprentice. Unless Samir hired more to tip the odds in his favor. Though it was possible, Parker believed the home field advantage, and a room filled with experts would be an effective balance. *Make your move.*

He had to give the entire setup praise for authenticity. The three men playing the parts of Franklin, Matt and Ray looked remarkably similar to his friends and comrades in Iraq. It was the equivalent of a dress rehearsal, and the finality of it all seeped into Parker, turning him numb from the inside out. Without Becca, warm and real beside him, he might have disappeared.

As those present shared memories of Theo in his various roles, Parker's mind carried him far from the quiet room and back into the heated combat zones they'd survived. He felt a nudge and glanced over to find Becca eyeing him with expectation as she tilted her head toward the podium. There too he was met with the expectant expression of Theo's older brother, his eyes puffy and red. The man was the bravest of them all today.

Parker walked to the front and turned to the small gathering. He had to play the part as well as the rest of them. He thought of the people he'd served with through the best and worst of military conditions. They all knew death was part of living and risk part of military service, but he found himself speaking to Becca.

He shared what Theo had meant to him. Not in

recent years or as part of Samir's revenge, but as a unique and strong-minded personality, as a competent and willing leader. He wasn't sure how long he spoke, only that he continued when his voice wanted to crack because Becca's gaze held his, giving him courage.

He returned to his seat and let her warm his chilled hand with hers until the service ended.

"No attack." He didn't bother to hide his disappointment from Becca. "So much for being an irresistible target."

She slipped her arm around his waist as the others moved out to secure the room until they could clear the weapons. "I find you irresistible," she said.

Her quirky humor made the failed plan easier to bear. Becca's resiliency had captivated him from the moment she tried to shove his boot out of her door. Had it only been a few days? Another round of checks in his ear claimed no sign or sighting of Samir or his accomplice.

"I was sure this would draw them out." He loosened his tie and unbuttoned his collar as they walked toward the hotel where David and the others were staying, according to Sam's maneuvers. He wasn't afraid of being on the street with her, knowing the SFPD and the FBI had spotters all over.

"Did we scare him off?"

"Possibly. None of this is making sense." Parker sighed. "I shouldn't be surprised. He's made a study of being unpredictable since he put this in motion."

Suddenly there was shouting and chatter on the comms from the surveillance teams. A fire alarm went off at the hotel. Parker and Becca exchanged a glance and broke into a run up the block.

Keeping her safe was essential, and he looked around for someone he trusted to hand her off to while he went after Samir. Everyone was converging on the hotel, and when they joined the fray, they found the lobby teeming with every brand of law enforcement, including Detective Baird, who walked over immediately.

"Did you see him?"

"No." Parker's stomach clutched. "What happened?"

"We've got the accomplice upstairs," Baird said. "Attacked the agent playing Franklin."

"And Samir?" Parker demanded.

The detective swiveled toward the front doors. "He should have passed right by you."

"I'll find him." He'd studied the area, chosen this place because of the escape options for Samir. He gripped Becca's shoulders, firmly. "Stay with the detective." Kissing her forehead, he bolted for the door before she could argue.

BECCA WATCHED HIM GO, wishing she'd found a way to keep him out of town and away from trouble. Last night had been the best of her life. She didn't want to contemplate that it would be the only night with the man she loved.

Loved.

She turned the word around in her mind, still not sure how or when she'd started to fall for him. During her initial background search? Looking into his eyes for the first time at her door? Maybe in the dark of the safe room, when she'd all but known Parker was holding her. Any and all of those moments had solidified into an emotional certainty. She'd fallen with no chance of recovery when they were in the darkness of his grief, and he'd finally been brave enough to open up. To her.

She ran her fingers up and down the strand of pearls. She loved the man and he'd gone charging out after a vengeful assassin. "Who has his back?" she asked the detective.

"I'm not sure. We have spotters and cameras all over the area."

"Right. And who has eyes on Parker?"

She'd told him that he didn't have to finish this alone, that he had backup. She would damn well be sure it was true. She followed the detective to what appeared to be a staging area of sorts in the hotel security office. Sam was there, furiously working on camera angles.

She wedged her way closer to Parker's friend. "Do you see him?"

He shook his head.

She stifled the frustrated scream, watching the various images for any glimpse of Samir or Parker.

"There." She pointed and Sam did something to magnify the view. She'd seen little more than a shadow moving through the construction zone across the street, but she knew Parker's build and the way he moved.

"Are you sure?" Sam asked.

She was. As far more qualified people around her debated and assessed, Becca slipped out to do whatever she could to save the man she loved.

Rushing across the street, she ducked through the fence surrounding the scaffolding. Hearing the sounds of a fight several stories up, she cringed and started up the stairs. She didn't focus on her lack of weapons or skills. She trusted her ability to create a distraction that would give Parker an opening.

When she reached the floor, she hit the lights and tucked herself low, hoping she wouldn't be seen yet as she peered through an opening. The men broke apart for a moment, both of them raising an arm to shield their eyes. Parker was on one knee, breathing heavily. Samir breathed hard as well as he rolled to his feet.

"Who's there?"

Now that she saw the scarred face, she recoiled. If not for Parker, she might still be Samir's captive. Or worse. Though fear left her trembling, she would not back down or leave Parker to handle this alone.

"Your accomplice is in custody," she shouted. "Give up now."

"Get out of here, Becca!"

"Help is coming," she called out. They had to be closing in.

Samir turned to run, but Parker lunged after him and tackled him, driving him farther from her. They were exchanging punches and kicks and getting dangerously close to the edge of the construction where only plastic sheeting guarded the long drop-off.

He couldn't believe jumping was an option, could he?

"I brought your money," she shouted at Samir's back. "Take it and escape. Go home while you can still leave the country."

Samir pulled a knife on Parker and drove for his midsection. Parker feinted, his jacket getting sliced in the process. As he dropped and rolled away from another swing of that wicked knife, the loose fabric caught on a piece of equipment.

Samir went for a killing strike and missed. He cursed at Parker and raced for the stairs. "We are not finished."

"That's what you think." Parker leaped up and attacked again, heedless of the knife.

Becca covered her mouth as she watched the fight. The heavy blows and near misses were more than she could bear. Where was their backup?

"Let him go!" she cried, giving the performance of her life. Hearing a helicopter rotor overhead, Becca shouted at him again, "Take the money and go!"

When Samir hurried toward the stairs, she moved to block his escape. The man skidded to a stop, glancing over his shoulder as Parker closed in from behind.

"It *is* over," she said. If she could keep his attention, Parker would have room to seize the advantage. "You can't escape."

The assassin faced her, his mouth twisting into an ugly sneer. "I came to kill my enemies, not die on foreign soil."

"Plans change," she said, holding his attention.

"There is no honor among thieves, only power and respect," Samir said in his heavy accent. "To bring the head of the enemy to my people will restore my rightful place as leader."

She wanted to vehemently deny the idea of Parker fatally wounded here, in this skeletal construction zone. "There is no honor in murder, you freak."

Samir advanced. "I am justified. He is the killer!"

"You're a tyrant." She scooted back another few steps, buying more space for Parker.

"My *cause* is justified," he roared, pumping the knife into the air.

Under his raised arms, she saw Parker pick up a length of scrap metal. She held her ground. "Petty vengeance is not a cause."

He reached out, grabbing her by the strand of pearls. She leaned back, putting all her weight away from him. The necklace broke and she tumbled backward into the stairwell, hearing Parker's voice as the world faded to darkness.

Chapter Thirteen

One week later

Parker kept peeking at Becca, watching her carefully for any lingering sign of pain or distress during the drive to his cabin in Big Sur. He wanted to impress her, and despite the doctor's assurances, he wanted to be sure she was healthy enough to be impressed. Now that the danger was over, what he had to say could wait a little longer, if necessary.

Of course it had been too much to expect her to stay with the detective when he'd chased down Samir. He'd been by her side from the moment the ambulance had transported her from the construction site, only leaving her long enough to shower and change into clean clothes once a day. She'd been unconscious for thirty-six hours, the worst hours of his life. It had taken several attempts before his friends convinced him it wasn't all his fault she'd ended up in the hospital.

When she'd finally woken, sore and disoriented, her first word had been his name. It had done more to heal him than all the legal fallout and justice combined. As she recovered, Lucy and Rush and Sam and Madison had all stopped by to keep them company and commend her for her bravery.

Eventually he'd explained Samir had committed suicide by law enforcement, refusing to surrender when he was surrounded, and by charging the officers he'd sealed his fate. With the cooperation of the accomplice, the FBI and other authorities were piecing together all the clues to the Iranian's crimes— from the original email and blackmail note to the assaults and murders.

He parked in front of the cabin and hurried around to open her door and help her out.

"I'm not fragile," she promised, but she didn't shrug off his assistance.

"I've never brought anyone else here," he said, throwing open the door to his private retreat.

"Oh, Parker." Becca immediately moved through the space, complimenting various things along the way until she reached a wall of glass with a western view of cliffs and ocean.

"You like it?"

She shot him a look over her shoulder. "You knew I would." She stood at the window, her hands rubbing some heat into her arms. The sunset on the other side of the wide bank of glass caught the fiery highlights in her hair. "The view is gorgeous. I don't know how you drag yourself away."

"I've been tempted to hole up here and live like a hermit." Thank God he hadn't done so or he never would have found her.

The temperature had dropped on the drive, and the forecast called for a cool night. To Parker it made the perfect excuse for cozying up to the fire. He knelt by the fireplace, and once the kindling caught, he joined her at the window, wrapping his arms around her waist. Giving her his warmth until the fire chased the chill from the air.

"I first saw this place in late afternoon," he said. "The Realtor and I walked the property first and then the sun was just starting to set when we stepped inside. I think he did it on purpose to get the sale."

"Smart Realtor," Becca said.

"Definitely." Parker chuckled, remembering it fondly. "I should've known I didn't stand a chance. He was referred by Rush and Sam. They don't tolerate slow or second-rate in any area."

Through the years, the number of people Parker trusted with his life could be tallied on one short list.

He'd never expected to share his deepest thoughts or secrets with a woman. Of course he hadn't believed a woman like Becca—smart, funny and safe enough to trust—existed.

He'd treated her badly, yet every chance she had to turn on him, she'd turned toward him instead. He wasn't sure he would ever really be worthy of her, but he wanted to spend a lifetime trying.

"Becca." He turned her away from the view, and when he looked into her big blue eyes, all the things he wanted to tell her jammed up inside his head. He dropped his forehead to hers and just breathed her in. She was alive. They were alive.

It was time to take the next step. Well, it was time to *ask* her if she was interested in taking the next step with him. No more issuing orders or fighting for control. He wanted her in his life, as his equal partner in all the days to come.

He nearly swore when the sapphire-and-diamond ring in his pocket seemed too heavy. How was it he could blow a hole in an enemy stronghold with confidence and the idea of popping the question had his knees knocking? He knew it wasn't second thoughts or cold feet. He was entering uncharted territory.

"Becca, thank you for coming up here with me."

Her generous mouth spread into a wide, happy smile that made her eyes sparkle. "We deserve some time to recoup and recover, just the two of us."

Her words warmed his heart, steadied him. "We do," he agreed. "This place means something to me and I wanted to share it with you."

Her auburn eyebrows arched toward her hairline at his admission. "Thank you."

"You know, after handling the earlier, um, situation so badly."

Her blue eyes twinkled with amusement. "We're both past that now, right?"

"Right. I just—I mean." He clamped his mouth shut. He would not stammer and bumble his way through a marriage proposal. He leaned in and kissed her. Her lips, soft and yielding beneath his, settled his racing thoughts. When he lifted his mouth from hers, the words tumbled out exactly as they were meant to. "Becca Wallace, would you please be my wife?"

"Oh, Parker." Her eyes glistened with emotion and then her gaze dropped to the ring he held up for her.

Although the blue sapphire reminded him of her eyes when she laughed, he suddenly worried that he should have chosen a traditional diamond ring. "If you don't like it, we can—"

She pressed a finger to his mouth to silence him. "It's a beautiful ring. Perfect." Still, she didn't take it.

Was that a no or a yes? Would it be pushy to ask for clarification? If other men had this much trouble, they sure didn't tell anyone about it. "Is it too soon?" He pulled the ring back. "Can you forget I asked? We'll just take it a day at a time." He should've known it would take more time to win her over. They'd been through too much.

"Hang on." She caught his hand, her eyes on the ring for a long moment before she raised that gaze to his. "Parker, I knew you, I fell in love with you in the dark." She lifted his free hand and pressed a kiss to the center of his palm.

The move sent a tremor through him, stole his breath, just as it had done the first time when they were on the beach, watching a different sunset.

"I love you, Parker. You can count on me to always stand by you forever. Yes! My answer is yes." She bounced a little on her toes. "I can't wait to be your wife."

Her words, the sincerity in her vivid blue eyes smoothed away the last of the rough edges, even before she kissed him tenderly. At the sweet, familiar contact, he felt everything inside him click into place like the proverbial key in the lock.

"I love you, Becca. No matter what has been or what will be, you'll always be my light." He guided the ring onto her finger, where it sat, a perfect fit, just like the two of them.

* * * * *

*Can't get enough of bestselling duo
Debra Webb & Regan Black?
Check out MARRIAGE CONFIDENTIAL
and INVESTIGATING CHRISTMAS,
available now from Harlequin Intrigue!*

I N T R I G U E

Available November 21, 2017

#1749 ALWAYS A LAWMAN
Blue River Ranch • by Delores Fossen
Years ago, Jodi Canton and Sheriff Gabriel Beckett were torn apart by a shocking murder and false conviction. Can they now face the true killer and rekindle the love they thought they'd lost?

#1750 REDEMPTION AT HAWK'S LANDING
Badge of Justice • by Rita Herron
The murder of her father has brought Honey Granger back to her small Texas town, but despite his attraction to Honey the hot Sheriff Harrison Hawk has his own motives for looking into her father's death—the disappearance of his sister.

#1751 MILITARY GRADE MISTLETOE
The Precinct • by Julie Miller
Master Sergeant Harry Lockheart was the only survivor of the IED that killed his team—but he credits Daisy Gunderson's kind letters to his actual recovery. And now that he's finally met the woman of his dreams, he's not about to let a stalker destroy their dreams for the future.

#1752 PROTECTOR'S INSTINCT
Omega Sector: Under Siege • by Janie Crouch
When former police detective Zane Wales couldn't protect Caroline Gill, he left both her and the force behind, unable to face his failure. But now that a psychopath has Caroline in his sights, can Zane find the courage to face the past and protect the woman he loves still?

#1753 MS. DEMEANOR
Mystery Christmas • by Danica Winters
Rainier Fitzgerald manages to attract both a heap of trouble and the attention of his parole officer, Laura Blade, only hours after his release. Can the two of them crack the cold case on Dunrovin ranch or will Christmas be behind bars?

#1754 THE DEPUTY'S WITNESS
The Protectors of Riker County • by Tyler Anne Snell
Testifying against a trio of lethal bank robbers has drawn a target on Alyssa Garner's back, and the only man who can save her from the crosshairs is cop Caleb Foster, who harbors secrets of his own...

YOU CAN FIND MORE INFORMATION ON UPCOMING HARLEQUIN® TITLES, FREE EXCERPTS AND MORE AT WWW.HARLEQUIN.COM.

Get 2 Free Books,
Plus 2 Free Gifts—
just for trying the Reader Service!

YES! Please send me 2 FREE Harlequin® Intrigue novels and my 2 FREE gifts (gifts are worth about $10 retail). After receiving them, if I don't wish to receive any more books, I can return the shipping statement marked "cancel." If I don't cancel, I will receive 6 brand-new novels every month and be billed just $4.99 each for the regular-print edition or $5.74 each for the larger-print edition in the U.S., or $5.74 each for the regular-print edition or $6.49 each for the larger-print edition in Canada. That's a savings of at least 12% off the cover price! It's quite a bargain! Shipping and handling is just 50¢ per book in the U.S. and 75¢ per book in Canada.* I understand that accepting the 2 free books and gifts places me under no obligation to buy anything. I can always return a shipment and cancel at any time. The free books and gifts are mine to keep no matter what I decide.

Please check one: ☐ Harlequin® Intrigue Regular-Print   ☐ Harlequin® Intrigue Larger-Print
                            (182/382 HDN GLWJ)   (199/399 HDN GLWJ)

Name _____ (PLEASE PRINT) _____

Address _____ Apt. # _____

City _____ State/Prov. _____ Zip/Postal Code _____

Signature (If under 18, a parent or guardian must sign) _____

Mail to the Reader Service:
IN U.S.A.: P.O. Box 1341, Buffalo, NY 14240-8531
IN CANADA: P.O. Box 603, Fort Erie, Ontario L2A 5X3

Want to try two free books from another line?
Call 1-800-873-8635 or visit www.ReaderService.com.

*Terms and prices subject to change without notice. Prices do not include applicable taxes. Sales tax applicable in N.Y. Canadian residents will be charged applicable taxes. Offer not valid in Quebec. This offer is limited to one order per household. Books received may not be as shown. Not valid for current subscribers to Harlequin Intrigue books. All orders subject to approval. Credit or debit balances in a customer's account(s) may be offset by any other outstanding balance owed by or to the customer. Please allow 4 to 6 weeks for delivery. Offer available while quantities last.

Your Privacy—The Reader Service is committed to protecting your privacy. Our Privacy Policy is available online at www.ReaderService.com or upon request from the Reader Service.

We make a portion of our mailing list available to reputable third parties that offer products we believe may interest you. If you prefer that we not exchange your name with third parties, or if you wish to clarify or modify your communication preferences, please visit us at www.ReaderService.com/consumerschoice or write to us at Reader Service Preference Service, P.O. Box 9062, Buffalo, NY 14240-9062. Include your complete name and address.

She had died here. Temporarily, anyway.

But she was alive now, and Jodi Canton could feel the nerves just beneath the surface of her skin. With the Smith & Wesson gripped in her hand, she inched closer to the dump site where he had left her for dead.

There were no signs of the site now. Nearly ten years had passed, and the thick Texas woods had reclaimed the ground. It didn't look nearly so sinister dotted with wildflowers and a honeysuckle vine coiling over it. No drag marks.

No blood.

The years had washed it all away, but Jodi could see it, smell it and even taste it as if it were that sweltering July night when a killer had come within a breath of ending her life.

The nearby house had succumbed to time and the elements, too. It'd been a home then. Now the white paint was blistered, several of the windows on the bottom floor closed off with boards that had grayed with age. Of course, she hadn't expected this place to ever feel like anything but the crime scene that it had once been.

Considering that two people had been murdered inside.

Jodi adjusted the grip on the gun when she heard the footsteps. They weren't hurried, but her visitor wasn't trying to sneak up on her, either. Jodi had been listening for that. Listening for everything that could get her killed.

Permanently this time.

Just in case she was wrong about who this might be, Jodi pivoted and took aim at him.

"You shouldn't have come here," he said. His voice was husky and deep, part lawman's growl, part Texas drawl.

The man was exactly who she thought it might be. Sheriff Gabriel Beckett. No surprise that he had arrived, since this was Beckett land, and she'd parked in plain sight on the side of the road that led to the house. Even though the Becketts no longer lived here, Gabriel would have likely used the road to get to his current house.

"You came," Jodi answered, and she lowered her gun.

Muttering some profanity with that husky drawl, Gabriel walked to her side, his attention on the same area where hers was fixed. Or at least it was until he looked at her the same exact moment that she looked at him.

Their gazes connected.

And now it was Jodi who wanted to curse. Really? After all this time that punch of attraction was still there? She had huge reasons for the attraction to go away and not a single reason for it to stay.

Yet it remained.

Don't miss
ALWAYS A LAWMAN,
available December 2017 wherever
Harlequin® Intrigue books and ebooks are sold.

www.Harlequin.com

Need an adrenaline rush from nail-biting tales
(and irresistible males)?

Check out **Harlequin® Intrigue®**
and **Harlequin® Romantic Suspense** books!

New books available every month!

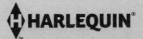

LOVE
Harlequin romance?

Join our Harlequin community to share your thoughts and connect with other romance readers!

Be the first to find out about promotions, news, and exclusive content!

Sign up for the Harlequin e-newsletter and download a free book from any series at

www.TryHarlequin.com

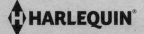
HSOCIAL2017

THE WORLD IS BETTER WITH

Romance

Harlequin has everything from contemporary, passionate and heartwarming to suspenseful and inspirational stories.

Whatever your mood, we have a romance just for you!

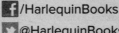